Fish Eyes and Lola

JANE LINDBORG

authorHOUSE®

AuthorHouse™
1663 Liberty Drive
Bloomington, IN 47403
www.authorhouse.com
Phone: 833-262-8899

Published by AuthorHouse   12/09/2020

ISBN: 978-1-6655-0707-3 (sc)
ISBN: 978-1-6655-0706-6 (e)

Library of Congress Control Number: 2020922127

Print information available on the last page.

This book is printed on acid-free paper.

"You can't put an old head on young shoulders."

~Christina E. Rumbaugh~1864 – 1937

"HEY FISH EYES!" Frank yelled. "Stay away from my sister!" "Shut up you honkey freak," Fish Eyes muttered under his breath as he pulled the bell on Lola's door. It flew open with a swish. Her soft pink lips spread into a wide smile, her white teeth sparkled. He wanted to stick his tongue deep in the middle of them.

"Hi Fish! What ya want?" she giggled. Her tight red shorts made him drool. The gardenia perfume she bought at Woolworth's drove him nuts. Everywhere she went it smelled like a fresh bouquet.

I want you Lola," he drawled. You wanna go for a coke?" He said coke since he didn't want to spend much. Out of the corner of his eye he could see her brother Frank coming their way. "Lola, yer sure scraping the bottom of the barrel messin' with that loser. You better wake up." He snarled. "Don't go givin' my sister any beer. You mess up my sister and I'll shoot your hillbilly ass!" Frank forced his way inside.

"What's wrong with yer brother?" Fish Eyes felt miffed. "I'm not such a bad guy. Let's go." "I'll tell ma I'm going for a coke, bye!" She didn't wait for an answer.

The malt shop was bustling when the young couple settled at the counter. Nervously, Lola whirled around and around on the stool. "Just like a merry-go-round," she snickered.

When the jukebox began playing Lola pulled on Fish Eyes to dance. "Naw, naw." His face went red. "I can't dance." Just then a smooth looking fellow floated up like soft lightening, slipping his arm around Lola's tiny waist, they sailed around the tables. Fish felt angry and jealous.

Edgar John Dailey was born in La Porte County, Indiana on a cold January morning to Mabel and Harry. They could not afford going to the hospital, so Mabel suffered on the couples' lumpy bed until their fourth child arrived all red faced and puckered.

Fish Eyes was pinned on him since his eyes were always large and rheumy. Edgar hated that nickname and endured many school yard fights, eventually it became his second name, and he learned to live with it.

Lola returned to him when the music stopped. She could feel perspiration under her blond curls and between her round breasts.

"I hate going home. I wouldn't care if I never did again," she sighed.

"You got any money?" Fish asked.

"Sure, a few bucks, who wants to know?" She looked ticked.

"I got a hundred dollars stashed out in my truck. How 'bout you en me drivin off into the sunset? Trucks gotta new battery." His voice cracked close to her ear. He breathed in her intoxicating perfume.

"Where'd we go? Ma would have a fit." Her blue eyes sparkled.

"Maybe go to a bigger town en git jobs. We'd have a ball."

"Oh, I'd like that." Lola wiggled close, sipping her drink. She kissed his ear, dribbling coke down the front of her white blouse. "They really don't need us. They'd get over it soon or later. We'd write, let èm know where we're at, stuff like that. We'd make money en come home for visits sometime," he assured her.

Lola leaned back on the stool as if she visioned them living in some honeysuckle draped town, with wanted workers signs in every storefront window.

"It would be easy leaving. Pa is an old crab. Smells like garlic and works all the time. I would miss ma.

"That's ok you can write her, call her whenever you want. We'll drive home holidays."

"Oh Fish!" That sounds like fun. Ya think we can?" She snuggled close and stuck her tongue in his ear. They squealed and wrestled at the counter.

"Cut it out you guys!" The soda jerk yelled. "If you want to fight, take it out in the yard!" "We'll just do that you sore ass!" Fish smarted back. Yanking Lola's arm they slogged out the door. Howling with laughter they climbed into his pickup truck. A soft summer breeze fumed through the open windows as they slowly drove towards home.

"Ma wants me to graduate. I hate school. Those cheerleaders are so uppity. Let me tell you those guys on the football team like me better than those snobs!" Lola set her jaw. "Give me a break. I don't want to go back home. I don't plan on washing dishes." She held her small white hands up to the moon. "I'm staying young and beautiful, not old like ma. No dishes for these hands."

"You don't have to." Fish Eyes sighed. "You go home en pack up all you can. Take what you need without letting them know. Ya could act like yer goin to bed. Meet me down the road by the pond. I'll be waitin. You better leave note so they don't worry. Bring some warm clothes; we might end up in Alaska." She slammed the ruck door and ran toward the house.

As Lola slipped upstairs to her room she heard Frank yelling. "Ma you better do something, she messin around with that Fish Eyes again. He's goin to knock her up. You mark my words!" Lola could not hear if her ma commented. She grabbed her toothbrush, face powder and Prell shampoo. After stuffing a satchel full of clothes, Lola tiptoed down the creaky stairs thru the kitchen and out the screened door. She was out of breath when she reached Fish Eyes waiting in the truck.

"Baby, ya made it! Anybody see ya? What ya bring." Shit, what ya bring them for?" Fish sounded disgusted spying a pair of white ice skates hanging by long laces around her neck. Lola opened the back of the truck and tossed her bag inside, then slammed the tailgate under the truck cap.

"Don't yell at me! They èr my skates. Someday we might find ice and I'll skate like a pro." Lola ran her fingers through her damp curls. "Where we going first?" She moved closer. Don't be pissed at me for bringing my skates. You did say we might end up in Alaska. We'll be like Bonnie and Clyde."

Fish reached over and patted her bare leg. "Ain't ya happy we're leaving this crummy little town?" I got us a big bottle of booze right here under the seat. Any stuff we want we always can lift."

"Fish, don't tell me you'd steal! Not me, that's one thing I won't do."

"Just wait en see what I can teach ya," he laughed. It's going to be all about you baby."

★

The dirt lane seemed to go on for miles before it ended deep in the forest. Smoke from the crude cooking pots curled high above the trees. Hounds tied to sheds barked and fretted in the shadows.

"Hey Wally what ya got?" A seedy fellow shouted.

"Got me a doe. Give me a hand." Wally grunted, puffing deeply as he dragged a deer carcass into the compound.

Ya ain't s'posed to kill deers in the summer are you?" A seedy fellow shouted.

"Who's lookin, we gotta eat don't we?" Wally wheezed. "Help me out. We gotta dress it down en fast." Women and children stepped closer to peer at the dead animal.

"Get me some hot water en rags. We gunna have one hell of a cookout."

"Mr. Gillie's coming!" a small boy shouted as an old black Harley shot through the opening spewing dirt and gravel, "Kill it, yer getten dirt on our supper!"

The burly man dismounted. Everyone backed aside as he lumbered over to watch Wally cut out the best parts of the doe. "You people better move fast, stop gawking. Get them fires started," Gillie bellowed. Quietly the bystanders immediately obeyed and took action.

★

I left ma a note en told her I wasn't running away, just looking for a little adventure. I told her I loved her and we'd come home sometime." Lola snuggled close to Fish as the truck purred along the highway.

"Yer not gunna drag me to Sunday school all the time like ma does. Frank don't mind, he likes a girl at church."

"You don't need to worry. What else did you bring besides yer stupid skates?" Lola socked his shoulder. "OH! Fish Eyes yer so mean. You just wait someday I'll show you what a good skater I am. I'm getting hungry. I brought a jar of peanut butter and took a loaf of bread. Ma's going to think she's losing her mind looking for her bread. Pa's going to shit-no precious Roman Meal with his eggs tomorrow morning." She snickered. "I'm getting tired it must be midnight."

"I got some blankets and pillows in the back. We can move our stuff to one side. Good thing I left the truck cap on the back." Fish belched.

"Why can't we stay in one of those roadside cabins? I need a bathroom. I need to wash my hair." Lola whined.

"We will sometimes. We need to save our money now." Fish Eyes pulled the truck off the road and parked under several large maples. A short time later you could hear Lola protesting. "Stop pawing me! I wanna sleep! I miss my ma. I miss my soft bed already!"

Fish took a deep swig of booze, rolled over and went to sleep. Soon everything was quiet in the back under the truck cap.

June twentieth broke with a splash of warm sunshine as Fish Eyes and Lola crawled out to face a new day.

"Where can I go to the toilet?" Lola tucked her blouse inside her wrinkled shorts. "My bladder is going to bust!"

"Go behind those trees." Fish pointed.

"Like hell I will!" she shouted.

"Git in, we'll look for a gas station. You can go there." He placed the booze bottle on the seat. "Fish Eyes! Ya better hurry. I can't hold it much longer. I need to set on the throne." She jumped in the truck and slammed the door.

At a Mobile station in the woman's restroom Lola brushed her teeth, then washed her hair in the wash bowl. Water and shampoo suds slopped about the tiny room. Sometime later she emerged with a clean face and dripping hair.

The summer sun was high and hot by noon. "You better stop and feed me." Lola grumbled. Her shorts were stuck to her butt from the sticky seat coverings.

"Break out the peanut butter." Fish kept his eyes on the road and sipped whisky from the bottle.

"No! I want real food and a coke. We had peanut butter for the last three times now. I didn't think you would be so damn cheap." She pouted. "I thought we'd go someplace exciting like Alaska. I wanted to skate."

"We still can, we only left yesterday. Maybe we'll go someplace that's got a real ice rink.

Keep an eye out for a diner." He sounded irritated. "We gotta hang on to our money till we get jobs."

★

Lola stared out the window. "I miss ma. I didn't know you'd drink all the time. "You can call her or write when we get settled." He patted her bare leg again. Fish breathed in the intoxicating smell of her perfume.

"Oh you are so sweet. I feel better now. I do aim to get a good job." She leaned back and hummed softly. "I do know what I don't aim to get."

"What's that?" Fish questioned, watching the road and tipping the bottle to his lips.

"I don't want to get false teeth or a double chin. I don't plan on washing dishes either." She held her soft hands up. "I'm staying young and beautiful, not old like ma. No dishes for these hands."

"Who's gunna do èm?" Fish sneered. "Not me. Hey, baby when am I gonna git a little kiss?" He looked lustfully at Lola.

"Oh tough, poor boy." She smirked. "You might get a French kiss if you'd feed me a decent dinner.

Ya mean if I took you to some fancy eatin place I'd get something more. You know what I mean and what I want."

"Dream on," she mumbled. "I'm savèn myself for when I get married."

Ya, right. That's not what I have in mind. How stupid are you girl? You know damn well what we'd be doing. Are you that naïve?" Fish could not believe she was such a prude.

"Oh, look! There's a restaurant. See that funny monkey on top. Let's stop! I'm hungry. I want a hamburger!" Lola begged.

"Ya, we can. First we'll drive up a little and take a look around. We can always come back." Fish Eyes wanted find a good spot to park the truck.

As night fell Fish Eyes and Lola searched along the highway for a good place to park for the night. Fish slowed the truck when he saw an opening to a dirt lane. A broken weathered sign lay in the ditch. He squinted trying hard to read one visible word. "It says Bog"

"What's a bog?" Lola stretched her neck.

"Bogs are usually a wet place. I think huckleberries or cranberries grow in bogs." Fish answered.

"I ate huckleberries but never cranberries." She sighed. "Ma makes good huckleberry pie, wish I had one now."

"This road looks pretty good, probably goes into a farmer's field. Maybe to moonshiners. I'd like some of that stuff." Fish licked his lips.

Slowly they proceeded down the rough lane. Quickly the scene changed. The truck jerked and rattled over ruts and stones. Low branches slapped against the hood, limbs hit the windshield.

"Where ya think it will end? It's too narrow, we can't even turn around." Lola whined.

"Oh, shut up, give me time." Fish sounded angry. His eyes itched; his arms ached as he fought to forge ahead. "You act like somebody's prize pony. You're not so hot. I could have anybody I wanted." He growled.

"What's going to happen? I'm scared." Lola sat on the edge of the seat. Odd noises floated through the truck's open windows. Jerking and rocking the pickup continued into the darkness ahead.

Oh, look! What's that? You see those eyes?"

"Probably a deer. Just shut up and watch the road for me!" He gritted his teeth as the truck's left wheel dropped into a deep rut causing Lola to bump her head. "Look! I'm bleeding!" She wailed. "This is no fun. You said we'd have fun. I wish I'd never left my ma." She sobbed.

"I think we got a flat tire." Fish shut the motor off. "Here take the flashlight, get out and see if it's down. Check all the others too."

"I ain't gettin out." She sniveled. "I'm scared. I want my ma."

"Get the hell out en look! If they are ok, I'll ram out of this hole. Check all four tires, let me know what ya see." Fish orders. "Now git!"

"I got shorts on, my legs will get all scratched up."

"Just do it!" Fish shouted so loud the veins in his neck stuck out. "I never thought you were such a mama's girl, you scaredy-cat!"

Hesitating, Lola slowly opened the truck door and shined the flashlight about the woods. Warily she slipped off the seat and set her feet on the ground.

"Git at it! Don't take all day," Fish Eyes yelled. "Tell me what ya see!" He took a quick swig of booze.

"Fish, looks like this wheel is in a big hole. The tires on this side look ok."

"Git around on my side! Are they up?" He bellowed. The headlights appeared dimmer. He wanted to get this finished before the truck's battery went dead. Fish felt agitated. "Hurry up!"

A hard thump hit the back of the truck. Fish Eyes heard a muffled cry. He figured Lola fell down. "Oh shit! What's wrong now? Answer me!" He shouted. Feeling provoked, Fish jumped out on the uneven ground, causing his ankle to twist, excruciating pain shot up his leg. "Lola, come here! I'm hurt!" He shouted, then moaned softly. Everything became silent except for the sound of a hooting owl and sticks crunching in the distance.

"Damn it woman! Get in here! Stop playing around!" He howled. I'm hurt." Fish Eyes felt sick to his stomach.

"I know you yer hiding back there under the truck cap." He bent down and untied his shoe, his ankle was swelling. He pulled himself back upon the seat, the throbbing pain eased. Now and then he would yell for Lola to forgive him, and come up and help him.

Fish knew she was beat. "I'll let her sleep. I'll tell her how much I love her. She's been so damn stubborn," he whispered to himself. "Maybe she'll have to drive till my foot feels better." Fish had felt weary of her grumblings. They had been together now for three days and he had not even gotten one stinking kiss yet.

Fish Eyes was jarred awake by birds chirping. Slivers of morning sun peeked through the forest. He yawned and stretched. The empty booze bottle rolled on the floor. Fish could not believe he had been asleep so long. He reached back and pounded on the truck window.

"Get up baby! We gotta get out of here!"

His ankle hurt as he stepped down. "Come on Lola, let's get goin!" To his astonishment Lola was not inside. Nothing had been disturbed. The flashlight lay dim in the dirt.

★

"Hey Wally! What ya got there?" Mr. Gillie called as the big man ambled up to a large steel cage located under tall oak trees.

"I got me a woman! Ain't she pretty. She's ornery as hell." He chuckled.

"Where'd ya git her?" Gillie poked a stick at Lola. Carefully he checked a rope holding the door shut.

"I was running a coon hound last night. Come up on 'em stuck in the road. Liked what I saw so I took her."

"Ya mean there's somebody else?" Gillie ogled Lola up and down. "How old are ya girl?" None of your business." Lola rubbed her scratched and bleeding lets. She was scared and dirty.

"If yer nice to us we'll be nice to you." Wally spoke softly through the steel bars.

"Let me out of here! It's against the law. This is America!" Her words were cold and calculated.

"Whos' law?" Gillie chuckled, his baggy skin wiggled. "We're the law back here girlie, so get used to it. Don't ever get smart with me you little bitch." He reached in and yanked her hair.

Across the yard voices could be heard as women and children placed steaming food on long wooden tables. Behind the trees several junky house trailers could be seen.

"Come to breakfast!" Someone called. Mr. Gillie and Wally left Lola and joined the others to eat out under the morning sun.

★

Back down the lane Fish Eyes was frantically trying to figure out what happened to Lola. He felt certain she had never slept under the truck cap and wasn't out in the woods relieving herself. Maybe she had walked out to the main highway. He remembered passing a tavern called the Drunkin' Monkey. Fish planned to get the truck turned around and go see. His sprained ankle pained at every move. As he gunned the motor the truck lunged ahead. His empty whisky bottle rolled under the seat.

To his surprise, the woods opened up into a large grassy field. Fish Eyes slowed to a crawl as he observed the scene before him. Three rusty house trailers, several tents and people sitting at rough-hewn tables. Cautiously he drove behind some brush and began to drive out when he spied Lola standing in a steel cage shaking the bars. Her face was white with fear.

"Fish! Fish! Get me out of here! I'm scared of these people!" She cried, tears streaming down her dirty cheeks. Frantically, she pulled at a twisted rope holding the cage door shut.

Fish was horrified at the sight of Lola in a cage. How can this be? People casually eating while she languished in terror. He was afraid they would see the truck. Suddenly the coon dogs started barking and lunging toward him. Wally and Mr. Gillie rushed to see what he was doing, just as Fish Eyes reached the cage. He positioned his body for a confrontation.

"What the hell ya think ya doin?" Mr. Gillie grabbed him by the neck. Wally untied the cage door and shoved him inside.

"Here my little pretty! I bet he's yer boyfriend."

"I'm taking yer girl to my bed tonight." Gillie smirked and growled, pointing his grubby finger at Fish.

Lola stuck up her nose, acting unconcerned she bit her lip. "I'm hungry and I'm sick of these shorts. Be a good boy and toss me my back outa that truck. Why'd ya have to put him in here? He's not my boyfriend!"

Mr. Gillie liked her spunk. She made him feel horny.

"How old are ya?" He asked for the second time exposing a mouth full of rotten teeth.

"How old do ya think I am?" she toyed.

"She could be older en she looks." Wally whispered over his shoulder.

"I'm going to graduate from high school soon." Lola held the bars twisting her body in a suggestive manner.

"Ooh." Wally moaned.

"You goin' to get my bag? I'm cold and dirty." Sand blew between the bars as she stared.

"Should I?" Wally asked Mr. Gillie.

"Ya, I don't see what it would hurt. I want her to feel good for tonight. I'll send you food, he can starve." Gillie tipped his head toward Fish cowering in the back of the cage.

"If I'm going to get out of here tonight, I need to wash up. I'm so dirty." Lola's voice sounded free from anxiety. "Get my satchel out of the truck."

"Here ya go cutie." Wally dropped her bag with a thud on the cage floor. "What the hell ya got in here? It's heavy as lead."

"None of your beeswax, girl stuff." She smarted back.

Wally's hands trembled as he pushed a pan of warm water inside the cage.

"Hey! Get this guy out of here while I bathe!" She yelled.

"Ain't he yer boyfriend?" Wally looked surprised.

"That weakling, hell no. He gave me a ride in his truck. Git him outa here!" Her words cut Fish deeply. He thought she cared for him.

"Go set in yer truck till she gets done." Wally twisted Fish's arm behind his back. I'll be watchin' you so don't get any bright ideas or you'll never see light again!"

"Ooh, get her washed good cutie." Wally tingled. His imagination burned thinking about her washing those fresh pink places it appeared no man had enjoyed yet. He planned to double cross Mr. Gillie, he would be her first.

"Git going before this water gets cold!" Lola bellowed, banging on the cage bars. As Wally walked away, Lola frantically dug through the satchel retrieving one ice skate.

"Fish, Fish!" she called softly. "Get ready, I'm getting out of here." Quickly Lola began rubbing the skate blade across the rope holding the door shut. When Fish realized what she was doing he sat watching behind the steering wheel.

Sweat appeared on Lola's brow, wet hair stuck to her face as she sawed. Her arms felt heavy, she struggled on.

Fish could hear a radio somewhere blasting out Hank Williams' "Cold-Cold Heart." He could see Wally tending the dogs as they howled and strained on their chains.

Lola was determined to get out before that nasty Mr. Gillie touched her. She could barely stand the thought. When Wally moseyed closer, Lola shouted. "Get away! I'm not done washing yet. Now git!"

Wally's face flushed as he tried to catch a glimpse. In his obscene mind, he imagined she was washing her small naked parts, not like Gillie's woman he shared with big gaping vaginas. He slipped away with high anticipation.

Lola's spirits lifted as the ice skate blade finally cut through the heavy rope. Frantically she ripped it apart and bolted out. "Start it up, let's go! Quick, let's go!" Lola cried, jumping into the truck. Fish gunned the motor, swung around and charged toward the mouth of the lane. Out of the corner of his eye Fish could see Wally drop the dogs' bowl and run toward the trailers.

Gillie rushed out the screened door cursing, tossing his cigar in the grass. He grabbed Wally by the neck. "You fool! How'd she get out?" he bellowed.

Lola grasped the dash-board as Fish Eyes fought to keep the truck out of dangerous ruts. "Why ya say I wasn't yer boyfriend? That was cold, really cold." Fish sensed a frosty relationship ahead.

I'm trying to survive! You are so stupid. Frank was right. It's took me three days to find out! She screeched.

Through the open window they could hear Gillie's old motorcycle roaring behind them.

★

The Drunkin' Monkey tavern had been open for three years. Vern was proud of his establishment. After suffering the loss of one leg and an eye in the war he wanted to keep busy enjoying the company of folks stopping for lunch and a drink. The war and its pain made Vern tough. Even with his disabilities he could hold his own in most situations. Several times to his displeasure he had to act as a bouncer and toss out unruly. His M.P duties in the army had taught him defensive skills. Tough as he appeared to strangers he was soft and gentle with Zoe, his wife, and their baby girl.

Zoe always fluttered about doing housework in a soft cotton dress and high heels. Vern often slipped upstairs to their apartment just to run his hand under her skirt and whisper in her ear, "mine."

Zoe often appeared on the landing outside their door to look down at Vern only to see him drinking a beer, reliving again his war experiences with a customer.

"We were taking Pork Chop Hill for the second time at night. All hell broke loose." Vern said. "I got hit by something in my eye. I crawled into a small cave to get my bearings. God! My head busted. It was so dark, I felt someone close by."

"Who's there?" I whispered.

"Me," a voice replied.

"Who's me?" I asked. It was a gook. That's what we called them, gave me his name, rank in good English. I got a bad eye, are you going to try en kill me?"

"No. I'm not killing." He answered as shells ripped the sky above us.

"How goes you speak English?" I asked.

"My father studied University Michigan. He don't want war. I don't want war."

"Nah, I don't either." When the One Fifty Five Long Toms slacked off, I went out to find a medic. Lost my eye en leg fighten on Old Pork Chop Hill. What a waste." He sighed. "That poor gook had a broken arm and lost his weapon. I wonder what happened to that poor soul. Lord only knows." Vern shook his head slowly and took another drink. "When I was wounded en discharged from the Army all I felt was good old Indiana pulling me home."

"Zoe moved back inside their apartment, she knew those stories by heart. Vern repeated them to anybody who would listen.

★

Frantically Fish Eyes fought to keep the truck on the lane. Lola watched thru the back window for Mr. Gillie coming on his Harley. If they could make it to the highway, maybe they would have a chance. "I'm so scared! I'm scared he will get me! Hurry!" She quivered like a frightened animal.

"Oh shit!" Fish slammed the brakes just as the truck smashed into a tree that had fallen, blocking their way out.

"What are we going to do? He's coming fast!" Lola jumped out of the truck and ran off into the woods. The magic of this adventure was totally gone.

"Come back! I'll lose ya!" Fish cried as Mr. Gillie roared up. His old nineteen thirty-nine motorcycle smelled of hot oil. It snapped and crackled cooling off.

"Git yer ass outa there!" He ordered as Wally stumbled up dragging Lola. "Take that hot chick back to my trailer, now!" Gillie yelled. "I oughta shoot you right here. I sure could use yer girl and this truck." He grinned.

Don't take her!" Fish cried. "She's mine!"

"Shut up you punk!" Mr. Gillie spit. "I could snap yer skinny neck with one hand!"

"Fish Eyes help me! Help me!" Lola cried.

"Fish Eyes." Gillie roared laughing. I'll fix your little Fish Eye." Like a shot Gillie smacked Fish to the ground. He howled in pain as everything went black.

★

As Wally pulled back through the woods toward Gillie's trailer she sobbed. "He will make me do bad stuff. Trembling Lola slumped down. Wally jerked her up dragging her among briers. Thin rivers of blood rand down her legs.

"Please, please stop!" Lola begged. Tears and mud covered her frightened face. "I ain't done anything bad like that before. You gotta help me. Get me away and

I'll be your friend. Please, I'll be your friend if you get me out of here." Lola slipped out of Wally's grip and slithered to the ground again. Most all buttons were torn off her dirty white blouse, exposing a lace bra. His mouth watered thinking she had never had a man, old Gillie would tear her apart. In his demented mind he felt she was insinuating he could have her first. The pull of his sexual desire for her outweighed his fear of Mr. Gillie.

"If I let you go, will you be my girl?" he grunted as she yanked her arms free. His ruddy face broke into an excited smile.

"Ya, I'll be your girl if you get me out to the big highway." Lola moaned, rubbing her bleeding legs. Wally grabbed her arm and headed toward the mysterious huckleberry bog. Once inside Lola could see high bushes laden with huckleberries. The marsh was difficult to maneuver in. She stopped on moss covered logs and fought not to fall into pools of murky water surrounding grassy humps.

"Ya gotta watch out for water moccasins, they like it in here. It might be easier gittin bitten by a snake than what Mr. Gille's gunna do to us if we get caught." Wally held Lola up before she slipped into marsh slime.

"Well we ain't getting caught. You better get me out to the road if you want me to be your girl." Lola cautiously waded through the mire.

Finding a dry spot near a clump of cattails, the weary pair flopped down to catch their breath. Lola looked up at the huge cumulus clouds. She secretly prayed they reached God and he saw her dilemma.

I'm so tired I could die." Lola slapped at mosquitoes sucking blood out of her scratched and bleeding legs. She bit her lips as not to cry.

"We gotta keep moving." Wally pulled her up on her feet. His bully scowl had disappeared.

"Are we lost?" She groaned. Seems we been going around in circles like was passed those small pines before."

"Them's some farmer's crop for Christmas trees. It shows we'er headed up for dry ground." Wally coughed a gnat out of his throat. "We ain't lost yet."

Lola picked a handful of huckleberries and popped them in her mouth. Birds fluttered out of the bushes where they had been feasting.

Wally stretched his neck to look. "I think that's the road through those bushes. He cocked his head to listen. "I hear cars. We need to find a dry place to wait till dark before we go out on the highway."

They both jumped as a gunshot cracked in the direction they had run from. I bet old Gillie shot yer boyfriend." Wally showed no emotion. Lola went pale, she told herself she couldn't deal with it. She had to think only of herself now.

"Where you going now since you left Mr. Gillie?" Lola trembled.

"I'll be goin where you go. We'll be together." His thin lips spread to a sickening smile. I'll take care of you. Your job will be to keep me happy."

"Bull-shit right," was her ragged whisper. Lola kept thinking about Fish Eyes. She feared Gillie had killed him. What a fool she had been leaving her dear mother for excitement with Fish. This must be how you feel when you realize you married the wrong man she thought. If Fish wasn't already dead she knew he would be if her brother Frank got hold of him.

Wally touched her arm and whispered, "Don't move." Like statues they watched as a long black snake crawled over Lola's bare legs. Her face distorted as if in pain, she held her breath as it drug its long slimy body across her skin to finally disappear under some bushes.

Lola jumped up screaming as if shaking off the morbid feels of its cold body sliding over her scratched and bleeding legs. "I'm movin out of here!" she cried, tripping through sphagnum, clawing her way to the higher ground.

"We need to wait till dark in case Gillie's on the highway watchin for us to come out." Wally called. He sounded afraid. "He'll kill me for sure. I've seen him kill before." Struggling, he caught up with Lola. His eyes bugged out as he ogled at her exposed navel.

Wally fumbled in his pants shaking his penis toward her. Lola recoiled. "Don't make me puke."

Just then another gunshot sounded in the distance.

"Oh God! I know now he shot Fish Eyes." Lola sobbed.

"Stop bawling. Ya don't know for sure." Wally squatted down and pulled a bloodsucker off his ankle. He thought once he got her away from here in some nice hotel he'd have her eating out of his hand. With all this trauma Wally wasn't sure he could even keep an erection.

★

Mr. Gillie watched as Fish sawed at the fallen tree blocking the road. When Fish slowed down Gillie shot a pistol near his weary prisoner's feet.

It was a dark and smoky sky by the time Fish dragged the last branches off the lane. His clothes were sopping wet with sweat, his legs were unsteady. He was weak from hunger.

Gillie drove Fish down to the highway then quickly turned around, heading back to the trailer.

"I can't wait to get at yer girlfriend tonight," he groaned. "Wally should be holding her for me." He let out a raspy chuckle. Fish felt faint, without strength to answer.

Several pots were cooking over open fires when they approached the campsite. "You get over here and get some grub. I've needed another helping hand around here. You'll do just fine!" Gillie growled.

After eating Fish Eyes lay down on a dirty mattress next to an old trailer. He didn't hear owls calling from the bog or notice a coyote lurking around the garbage pile left from supper. Fish was dead to the world. His mind was void of Lola's fate or plotting any scheme to escape.

★

Wally decided they should lay low in the bog until daylight. Lola secretly observed the sun sinking into the horizon. West, she thought, the way they had turned down that notorious lane. She locked that direction in her mind. After reaching the highway she would head to the right, west, remembering they had passed a tavern somewhere down the road.

Wally settled comfortably inside a tall clump of marsh grass. "How old ya say ya are?" He stretched his neck to peek out of his primitive nest.

"Seventeen! I told you before!" Lola snapped, rubbing her scratched legs. "You ever kill anybody?" She looked down in his face.

"What if I did? It don't matter. You don't have to worry. I'm crazy in love with you. I saw Gillie kill a couple of times." Wally yawned again. Lola didn't ask any more questions.

"What's my poor little duck you scared of me? I ain't going to hurt you, we are a team. We gotta get out of here and do some hot lovin. Come over here and lay by me." He yawned and rubbed his eyes.

Lola sat down and tied her wet shoes on tighter. To her surprise Wally was snoring, his head rolling back in the turf. She had to make a quick decision. Darkness was setting in fast. Now and then heat lightening fluttered across the sky. Lola tried to gather her thoughts, she needed to settle down and not panic if there was a chance of her getting away from Wally and his lecherous plans.

Lola leaned closer, taking one more peek to be sure he was fast asleep. "Wally," she spoke. "Are you awake?" She cocked her ear and watched his chest rise and fall in a deep sleep. Now was her only chance to escape. Quietly she crept away.

The marsh held ghostly shadows. The night felt dense and unknown. Lola feared strange animals roaming about. Wally had spoken about wild hogs and catamounts back here.

Struggling through knee-deep muck, Lola headed for another rise of higher ground. It was dark now, her ears played tricks, thinking Wally was walking behind her. Fear gripped her aching body as she crawled on her hands and knees, clawing up the last ridge before reaching the asphalt highway.

Barely able to stand, Lola paused to get her bearings. Her eyes felt out of focus, itching, burning like full of cobwebs. Her heart pounded as she started running. Darkness distorted the roadway ahead. She felt she was running in place. Lola prayed Wally was still back in the bog sleeping like baby Moses in the bulrushes.

Smells of rotting vegetation from the swamp was thankfully disappearing from her nostrils. Lola's *bare feet made slapping noises as she ran. Her torn red shorts kept slipping down. She still worried Wally was coming behind. Her throat tightened.

Headlights were fast approaching from the back. Her best odds were to lie in the ditch until it passed. She did not want to chance getting into a car with another pervert. Lying in the gully, Lola was so tired she felt like never getting up. She had lost all track of time since she left her dear mother. Every bone in her body hurt, she felt faint from hunger. Lola blinked to regain her sight. Mud and sedge stuck in her hair.

Scrambling out of the ditch Lola could see the tavern ahead. She clearly saw a neon monkey on top the building, somersaulting over and over with a beer mug in his hand. She staggered on, blood dripping from her nose, soaking the front of her ragged white blouse.

"God help me, help me," she breathed.

★

Nine-thirty at night, Vern's' customers were still at the tavern. Six men in the corner playing poker. Small piles of coins were scattered around the table. Four guys were having a rowdy game of pool. Vern worked behind the bar filling their requests. He knew these men, all hardworking tax payers. Vern looked over at David enjoying a game of darts. His wife works nights at the hospital. David would play a couple games, have a beer or two, then go home and wait for her. Vern watched Bailey over at the card table. What a fine fellow, he though. Baily was a fireman. Two years ago he had fallen through the roof at the hardware store. His little girl often has nightmares about her dad and fires. There was Jon, owned a pottery shop and kiln stuck on the edge of his property. Vern enjoyed promoting his creations. He kept directions to Jon's shop for when tourists stopped at the tavern.

The door opened and Charles came through. Men looked up from their games and shouted. "Get your money out Charlie, we'll show you how to play poker." Noah the local electrician yelled, "where'd ya get that sissy pink shirt?" "Mother-in-law." Charles grinned. The boys knew he was no sissy. All one had to do is look at his muscular arms. "Vern tell Joe to cook my dog up a big juicy hamburg, no onions, just cheese. He's out in the truck. I told him I'd bring him out a burger — he's waiting." Charles called out and waves at Joe.

"What kind of dog you say he is?" Vern asked, wiping off the bar.

"He's a Catahoula Leopard Australian Sheppard, smart as a whip!"

"I never heard of that kind. I fed a scrawny mutt when I was station in Korea. Wish I could have brought him home. Probably somebody ate him. Poor people were hungry." Vern called again to Joe the cook in the kitchen. "Charlie wants that burger for his dog. He's out in the truck."

"I'll have a beer, been hauling logs all day. I'm dry." Charles pulled up to the bar with Noah.

The tavern would stay open until midnight. As much as Vern liked these men, he could not wait to leave the cleanup to Joe and go upstairs to Joe and the baby.

★

Darkness engulfed Lola as she ran. Stumbling toward the 'Drunkin' Monkey! Her lungs ached, she felt they were exploding. A heavy fog rolled over the building ahead. She blinked to make sure it was real, not her imagination. Lola limped into the parking lot, taking one last look behind, expecting Wally to grab her.

When Lola tripped and fell against a truck, the large dog inside lunged, barking, and clawing at the windows. She jerked back as if touching a hot stone. Staggering ahead she hobbled up the steps, pushed open the heavy wooden tavern door. Everything went black as she fell inside.

The men jumped from their games and rushed over to see a dirty, bleeding, ragged girl lying on the floor.

"Who are you?" Vern yelled. The puzzled men hovered about. "Anybody seen her around here before?" He looked up as they shook their heads. "Go get Zoe!" Vern yelled as Joe dashed out of the kitchen. "Bring a blanket!"

The astonished men stared down at the pitiful looking girl sprawled in front of them. She looked ghostly pale, with insect bites and scratches. Heavy dirt could be seen pushing under her torn fingernails.

Zoe came running down the stairs. "What's this?" She bent down. "Who can she be? Joe call the sheriff!" Lola was delirious, slapping out and kicking. She stared, looking at something no one else saw.

"Get away, get away!" don't touch me," she cried. Her eyes rolled back.

Zoe pulled Lola's blood spattered blouse shut covering her exposed breasts. "There, there, there, no one's going to hurt you." Zoe spoke softly and covered her with a blanket.

Lola opened her swollen eyes and looked at the men above her.

"You guys back up and give the girl some air." Charles removed his pink shirt, rolled it up into a pillow and carefully placed it under her head.

"We got to find out who she is," Vern whispered. After a while Lola attempted to sit up. She clutched the blanket around her. "OH! OH! I made it," she stammered. "I made it."

Zoe told Joe to bring the girl a cup of warm broth, not to hot.

"Who are you?" Where'd you come from?" Zoe questioned.

"Swamp, in the swamp! They had me in a cage back there." Lola covered her face and sobbed.

"In a cage?" Zoe's voice trembled. She looked up at Vern. Joe brought a cup of warm broth and carefully held it to Lola's lips. "I called the sheriff. He's on his way."

The men talked among themselves, wondering who she was. "We never seen her around her." Noah remarked. The others fully agreed.

Lola was sitting at a table, wrapped in a blanket when the sheriff came huffing through the door. "What we got here, Vern?" he asked, looking down at Lola. "Who are you young lady? Have you been molested?"

Lola shook her head no. "I'll tell you everything, just don't let them get me!" She sobbed.

"Who's them?" The sheriff looked stern. Wally, Mr. Gillie, those bad people back there in the bog. Fish Eyes is back there. I think Gillie shot him."

"Who in the hell is Fish Eyes? He tried not to laugh.

"A friend. We came from Three Oaks. We was just going away for a little adventure. I was such a fool. They locked me in a cage." She covered her face again with the blanked.

"I always suspected shit going on back there." Vern shrugged. "Some hard lookers stoop in here once in a while. You know they hold a big sale each summer. I think that's when they make their money."

"You think we should take her to the hospital?" Joe questioned.

"No! No hospital," Lola cried. "I need some food and sleep. I don't have any money, but when I feel better I can work to pay you back. I want to get back to my mom." She sighed.

"Where's home?" The sheriff asked again.

"Three Oaks, Michigan," she replied.

"We can take care of her till she can go home." Zoe pulled Lola's hair back and secured it with a rubber band. "We won't anybody get you."

It was past midnight when Vern locked up. The sheriff called out as the men were leaving. "Fellows, keep this quiet so can catch these jerks and find out what goes on back there in the bog."

Vern went off to bed while Zoe washed Lola's hair and fixed her bath.

"I think we should burn your clothes, I have things you can wear. I'm not much bigger than you." Zoe smiled. "Some of these cuts on your feet look pretty bad."

As Lola drifted off to sleep, she wondered what Wally did when he awoke and found her gone.

★

Lola awoke early. She felt sad thinking Fish Eyes was dead, but was so happy she had escaped from those horrible people.

Zoe tapped on the door. "Come and eat with us. Joe's got breakfast ready!" The rule was Joe did all the cooking for their home and tavern. Zoe did all the cleaning and laundry. Vern takes care of all the business. It opened at ten o'clock and closed at midnight. Close behind the tavern stood Joe's cottage.

Zoe, Vern and the baby entered, followed by Lola. She was reticent but grateful to be free and safe with these people.

The table was set, food was placed.

Everyone took a seat as Joe poured coffee. "Do you drink coffee?" He asked her.

"I haven't yet. I think it would be a good time to start." She smiled. Her cuts, scrapes and bruises were visible.

"That' a girl!" Vern chuckled. "Hot coffee can heal most woes."

Vern and Zoe trusted Joe with both family and business. He had come to them right out of high school asking for a job. After proving to be a dependable, trustful employee, Vern had offered this cottage as part of his pay.

Joe was a fine young man and pleasing to look upon, with his soft smile and twinkling eyes. Zoe and

Vern liked his quick humor. Nothing was slipshod with Joe. In summer he grew a fine garden full of greens, tomatoes, herbs and flowers. Often he prepared special recipes for the family. Vern and Zoe felt blessed to have him as an employee and friend.

Vern watched Zoe feed their baby. Love for his wife as deep. The only thing she ever did to get his goat as vacuuming under the bed while he tried to take a nap. Other than that, to him she was perfect.

★

Fish stirred and raised upon his elbows. His eyes burned, his mouth was dry. It took a few seconds to remember where he was as his mind cleared, it flew back to Lola. Where was she? The last time he had seen her she was crying to him for help as Wally was dragging her away.

Fish struggled to stand. His bones ached. He had had slept soundly all night. Near the wooden tables several women and children prepared breakfast in the bright sunshine.

Mr. Gillie came busting out of his trailer door straight at Fish. "You're in big trouble boy! I can't find Wally and the girl!" He roared.

"Why me? I was with you right here." He shouted back. "Not my fault you can't find èm."

"Git over here, we gunna have some grub." Gillie motioned. "Don't think yer gunna leave, I'll shoot ya next time."

Fish wanted to wash his face and hands. "Got any water?"

"Ya, there's a pump over there, do it. I'm watchin."

"Fish Eyes gulped down his food, scraping his plate clean. This was the first real meal he had had since all those peanut butter sandwiches with Lola.

"How'd you like to work for me?" Gillie forked a piece of meat into his mouth. "I'd pay ya, feed ya good. You could even sleep with one of my women. I bet you'd never have to be locked up again."

"Where's Wally?" Fish asked.

"Looks like he took off with that girl of yours. He better have a good excuse or I'll kill the bastard." His mean eyes narrowed.

Fish knew he meant every word.

After the tables were cleared, Fish and several other men remained smoking weed. Suddenly out through the edge of the bog Wally came staggering.

"Where the hell ya been? Where's my girl?" Gillie bellowed.

"I'm sorry boss, she gotta way. I looked all night. I was bringing her back to you and poof she just vanished. I'm afraid quicksand got her. I tried my best, boss. She was a spitfire to hold on to." He flopped down on the grass. "I've been lookin all night." He lied. "Can I get something to eat, I'm starvin."

"Sure, go in, the girls will feed ya." Gillie seemed to believe his concocted story.

"Quicksand?" Fish was almost crying.

"Ya, quicksand. There's a spot out there you can bet it will take you down if you step in it. I used it once to get rid of some smart mouthed kid. It'll suck ya down in five minutes." Gillie coughed.

Fish shivered. Lola gone, he could not take it in. He knew he could never go back again without her. "I might as well stay and work for you. I can't ever go home." Tears rolled down his dirty face. "All this shit en I never got one stinking kiss!" He mumbled.

After Fish Eyes accepted Lola was gone forever, he began to feel part of this band of misfits. Mr. Gillie had stopped raging on Wally for losing Lola. Wally became more like a friend to Fish Eyes teaching him what they did back here in this settlement.

The annual flea market was coming up in a few weeks. Folks will come from all over the country to sell their wares. Mr. Gillie will collect a sizeable fee from each vendor. The gigantic sale includes produce, folk art, merchandise and animals of all kinds.

Fish wondered if he had heard correctly the sale of children. Mr. Gillie had promised Fish a substantial wage, if he worked hard and kept his nose clean. Wally told him about bonfires, booze, music and girls, plus all the illegal actions they could take place in after dark.

★

Some time had passed since Lola fell inside the tavern door all bloody and frightened. Her skin had healed, but her fear of Mr. Gillie and Wally never left. Zoe enjoyed her company. They often worked and laughed together. Zoe felt comfortable allowing Lola to take the baby out in the back yard full of flowers and sunshine.

Joe stopped to chat as he left the cottage to work in the tavern. "What are you cooking today?" She asked, looking up.

I'm making meatloaf and mashed potatoes." He replied. "Zoe likes my meatloaf. I hope you will too." He smiled and tickled Chickie's tummy on his way by.

Lola felt grown up, responsible now. She realized what a selfish brat she had been. Lola was anxious to see her parents and apologize for all the problems she had caused.

Joe turned around. "Lola, would you do me a favor and wipe off my motorcycle? It's been parked all winter in the garage. I need to take it out for a spin. Maybe you would like to ride with me?"

"I'll have to ask Zoe first." She frowned. The sun felt warm on her back as she taught the baby how to patty-cake. She felt guilty thinking of all times she had sassed her mother.

That evening Vern told Zoe to send Lola down to help. "We had so many orders Joe can't keep up with the dishes. He had been shopping for a automatic dishwasher.

Lola was happy to feel normal again. She quickly combed her hair and skipped down the stairs.

By a little after midnight, Joe and Lola had put the kitchen in order, ready for the next day.

★

July was hot and dry. Things were buzzing back at the bog. Mr. Gillie's' big sale of the year was under way. Wally walked pompously shouting orders. He still could not grasp what had happened to Lola. He still couldn't grasp what had happened to Lola. He felt certain she wasn't in quicksand, but relieved Gillie fell for his phony story.

Wally observed what was being offered for sale. Hunting dogs, pigs, goats, and produce. Clothes, chicken and much more. Far away under the trees he knew three small girls held in the steel cage would fetch big bucks at night.

Fish Eyes emerged from an old trailer. He yawned, stretched and raked his fingers through his thick, dark hair. This is the life he thought, food and sex anytime he wished.

"Hey Fish! Git yer ass over here and give me a hand!" Wally yelled as he struggled to move a heavy table. "You better shape up and help out more or Gillie's gonna kick your lazy butt outa here!"

"Ya, ya, I'm coming." He tossed the dregs of his coffee in the grass, placed the cup on the step, Sometimes Fish yearned to return to Three Oaks, but what would he tell Lola's folks. Why would he leave this gravy train anyway?

The sun was up promising good weather for this two week long sale. It had stayed fifty-two degrees all night, keeping the mosquitoes busy. Fish Eyes instructed vendors arriving what to pay and where to park their campers.

Fish spied one of Gillie's women slide several plates of food toward the three caged girls. For a moment he felt sorry for them and knew it wasn't right. When Wally screamed at him for the second time, all compassion and common sense vanished.

★

Under the Hoosier moon, venders and vagrants anticipated the start of a promising bountiful sale. Stalls, booths, tables, pens and campers were busting with wares to begin at sunrise. Howling dogs, loud music bounced through trees spreading over drunken men in the grass.

In the big steel cage three tiny girls huddled, shivering and trembling with fear. Mr. Gillie had given orders to bring him the smallest one at midnight.

"Sure Boss, do I get one?" Fish Eyes asked, half smirking.

"Bring me more of that smooth whisky, me en you will drink to a night of sheer pleasure. Gillie slurred his words, Fish could barely understand.

Smoke from a hog roasting rolled over frenzied dancers. A fiddle wailed in the distance. "I hope police don't come back here." Wally sounded nervous.

All three men lolled on a grassy plot in front of the trailers. Gillie's women shuffled about smoking. Every now and then one called out for another drink.

Fish Eyes was sexually aroused thinking about Wally bringing them each a little girl. Deep down he knew it was wrong, criminal. He would have to decide when the time comes. No one noticed his ghoulish smile.

"We made a hell of a bunch of money and the sale hasn't even started yet." Wally sounded excited. "You boys do what I say en you'll get your share." Gillie stretched and rolled over on his back. "Look at them stars," he mumbled as a wave of smoke from the roasting hog swept slowly over them like a waving grey ghost.

"I can't wait to eat a slab of that pig." Fish smacked his lips.

"I can't wait ta git at one of them little girls, how about you Wally?" Gillie took another drink. "Tell my old ladies to go on to bed. We've got better stuff comin." Gillie rolled over in the grass and farted. "I ain't planning to sell èm till I get my fill!" He yawned and promptly began snoring.

Fish went to retch in the weeds. Nobody saw him fall down and pass out for the night with vomit stuck on his face.

Wally's head throbbed, he staggered inside a trailer and crawled in bed with one of Gllie's women.

★

The morning sun danced about Joe's cheery yellow and white cottage. He quickly set breakfast on as Vern's family and Lola arrived. Joe held the screen door open as everyone called out greetings.

"What do I smell?" Zoe tipped her head. "You people better be hungry. I've baked a load of sweet rolls." Joe held the chair for Zoe, then pulled up the highchair for Chickie Pearl. Vern shuffled on his prosthesis to the head of the table. Joe bowed toward Lola as he held her chair. As he bent close he could smell flowery shampoo.

"I think some of us ought to take a trip back to that bog sale and see what goes on." Vern dipped a sweet roll in his coffee.

"I don't want to go!" Zoe was adamant. "Those people would scare me."

Joe set a platter of fried mush and bacon in the middle of the table, with butter and maple syrup close by. From the stove he served poached eggs.

"Lola, would you want to go back there, if you were in disguise?" Zoe asked.

"Yes, I do want to find out what happened to Fish Eyes. If he is dead, I'd like to know where he is buried. We heard a lot of gunshots." Lola sighed. "I bet he is dead, they were mean."

"How long are you planning to stay here?" Joe asked Lola.

"After I get Fish Eyes' truck I'll go home." Lola looked over the table at Joe. She hated the thought of leaving these dear people.

"I'd say me and you go back on my motorcycle with a hat and sunglasses, maybe boy's clothes, nobody would know you." Joe suggested as he poured coffee. "Would you feel alright going back there dressed like that?"

"Yes, I want to find the truck. I want to feel under the dashboard for an envelope taped there. Fish claimed he had a hundred dollars in it. I want to get his truck so I can drive back home." Lola swallowed a lump in her throat. "Maybe I can find my clothes and skates."

"How close were you and this Fish Eyes"? Zoe asked as she unrolled a warm cinnamon roll. "You said his real name was Edgar."

"He was just a guy from the neighborhood. My brother Frank didn't like him one little bit."

"Why?" Vern asked.

"Frank said he was a looser." I was so dumb looking for a change. I didn't like school. Ma was determined I go. What a fool I was." Lola began to sob.

"You left with him 'cause you were a stupid kid. My grandma used to say, "you can't put an old head on young shoulders." Vern sighed. "Let's change the subject. That's all in the past for you Lola. You are a new girl."

"Oh yes sir I am!" She looked up through tears.

Vern lifted his cup. "Here's a toast to the new Lola. Thank God you came to our house. I think you should put on a disguise, go with Joe and find out what happened to Fish and the truck." Vern shook his head. "I've heard things.

"I'll look for my skates. I used a blade to cut through a rope. That's how I escaped them, then, that Wally caught me, "her voice strained.

"I've heard a lot of poly-foxen goes on back there." Vern tipped back in his chair.

Zoe lifted Chickie out of the highchair. "Lola we must get busy, Joe needs to start cooking for the lunch crowd."

★

The air-conditioned Drunkin' Monkey was a welcome oasis as patrons escaped ninety-degrees outside. Jon ordered a beer. Noah asked for whatever Joe was cooking. Jon ordered the same. Jon's wife was away teaching art classes in Indy, and he was starving.

"How's that little gal doing that came in here?" Noah asked.

"She's doing fine. A real nice kid. She's had time to think. Zoe takes good care of her." Vern smiled.

Several tourists stopped to eat and ask directions to the big sale.

"Just turn right out of the parking lot and you will see a sign about a mile. You can't miss a steady stream of cars been going in."

Plates of sausage, souerbrout, and mashed potatoes were ordered, along with Joe's special dessert "Blackberry Winter."

Some men came in hard hats, some in bib overalls, couples and a table full of linemen scattered about the room.

When Lola walked down from the apartment Vern put her to work washing dishes. Every time Joe darted in and out of the kitchen they smiled at each other. Lola felt very happy. She was truly a new woman.

★

The Drunkin' Monkey continually flashed on top of the building. Tip the glass, summersault, stand and take a drink, over and over the neon monkey did his tricks.

49

A fellow entered the tavern, stood and looked about. "Is that you, Sarge?"

Vern looked up from wiping glasses. "Well I'll be! Are you real or a ghost? Is that really you young Bob"?" Vern' face lit into a wide questioning smile as he rushed from behind the bar. Both men embraced, tears rolled down their ruddy faces. "It's been a long time, how'd you find me?" Vern held the man at arm length and studied his face.

"Young Bob, we made it! I didn't know if you was dead or alive. That Pork Chop Hill was sheer hell."

"Ya. I heard you was hauled off to Mash. Bob's voice quivered.

"Old buddy we got a lot of catching up to do." Vern limped over and drew two beers. He pulled out a handkerchief and wiped his nose. As David and Jon looked up, Vern called, "get over here and meet my old buddy!"

Vern grabbed two more drinks as they settled around the table.

"Ya, last time I saw Sarge medics were hauling a bleeding mess off to a mash. I figured he was dead."

How'd you find me?" Vern asked.

"Through the grapevine. I keep in contact with some guys from our unit. Somebody knew about you here in Indiana." Bob leaned back in his chair. "That

Vern was a hell of a Sarge. I heard you carried some poor G.I. with frozen feet for a mile to find a medic."

"Yes, then this happened, blew my pinkies off!" Vern shook his head. "Goodbye leg. He flicked his fingers. "My eye is another story."

"Well Sarge, you are a sight for sore eyes. Never thought I'd see you again!" Bob's eyes welled.

"Stay the night. We got a lot of catching up to do. I gotta get back to work. The lunch crew is coming."

Charles came through the door and called for a hamburger friend up for his dog in the truck. Somebody dropped money in the jukebox. Hank Williams belted out "Your Cheatin Heart." Vern felt happy, altho behind the bar tears rolled down his cheeks remembering the soldiers that had died that night and for his poor lost leg.

★

The morning Joe and Lola planned to snoop around the bog sale, Vern praised Joe for doing a superb job cooking and saving money for the business.

"My grandpa always said "A woman can waste more on a teaspoon than a man can bring in on a scoop shovel!" Joe chuckled. "Grandpa had three cures, fig bars, bleach and Vicks."

"I kept a jar of Vicks in my pack in Korea. It helped heal my cracked feet, then boom!" Vern sighed. "Who is this young lad at our table?" He teased Lola dressed as a boy.

"I hope those bad men don't recognize me." Lola felt apprehensive. "If Fish Eyes is really dead, I'm taking his truck. I know how to drive."

"Did you write your mother yet/" Zoe adjusted Chickie Pearl in her highchair.

"No yet, I will." Lola replied. "I'll tell her I'm well and happy and will be coming home soon. I'll tell her I'm the snotty kid she used to put up with. Folks here taught me to straighten up." She felt ashamed.

"You will do ok." Vern encouraged. "You have come a long way since you fell inside our door."

"Today is Sunday, we won't have to think about customers." Joe spoke softly. "We will go after I finish here."

"You sure look like a guy." Zoe smiled at Lola. They had tucked her blond hair tightly under a heavy hat. She wore thick boy's shoes, with a long sleeved plaid shirt and bagging blue pants.

The baby did not recognize Lola, she pulled away crying. Zoe comforted Chickie and remarked she was teething.

"The main thing is not to talk. It's strange how one's voice is as strong as a finger print sometimes. Let Joe do all the talking." Vern added. "Lola you sure could fool me in that getup. That penciled upper lip looks just like you are sprouting a mustache. You shouldn't wear perfume. I can smell you clear over here."

"This is the only perfume I ever wear. I thought I lost it running out of that horrible swamp." Lola felt stupid. "Maybe I should wash it off."

"It seems odd a tough guy like you smellin like gardenias." Vern laughed.

"Hard to tell there's a real woman under there." Joe's eyes twinkled as he looked at Lola. Her heart fluttered to have Joe call her a real woman. As Joe and Lola roared toward the bog sale on his blue Indian motorcycle, Lola was anxious to learn what had happened to Fish Eyes and his truck. Her stomach churned with the fear of seeing that horrible Mr. Gillie and Wally again.

★

Fish Eyes stood near the lane's opening taking fees from vendors. Every now and then he stuck bills down inside his socks instead of placing them in the money box.

Near the edge of the forest, Fish knew three small girls huddled inside the steel cage. His compassion disappeared when Wally called him to feed the hounds. He planned to go back to the trailer and take a nap. This high living of booze and women was taking a toll on his young body.

Smoke from grills rose like lazy grey silk above the trees. Wally strolled about begging for a taste of this and a piece of that until the vendors flatly refused. "If you wanna buy, that's what we are here for chum!" They snapped. "No more freebies!" Wally felt quarrelsome. Living here with Mr. Gillie no one ever said no to him. Anything from food to a woman was free. He still felt cheated for losing that pretty Lola. Sometime he planned to go back to the quicksand and look for her bones.

A seedy Mr. Gillie walked among the milling crowds. He turned quickly and shot an old Rhode Island Red rooster scratching in the sand.

"Hey! Stop! Dammit Gillie ya might a killed somebody!" Wally shouted.

"What if I did?" Gillie growled and spit, then shot another round in the air.

"You want those prick cops back here?" Wally picked up the unlucky chicken for the women to dress and fry.

Pungent bundles of dried lavender tansy, river weed along with mesh bags, filled with garlic bulbs and rose hips swung from tent awnings.

A group of men lolled under trees shooting dice and drinking beer. They rolled a muss melon on back and forth to the winner. It soon felt like the soft spot on a new baby's head. One looser got angry and busted it open. A goat wandered over and gobbled it down, rind and all.

An accordion sounded across the yard as crowds swelled around the water tank. A skinny woman with bad teeth questioned Wally about the little girls in the cage.

They are runaways. The father is comin to git ém." He lied. Wally knew the lucky man who bought them up under the elms loaded on ditch weed.

Wally was still angry at Mr. Gillie for shooting that old rooster without considering the police snooping around. He planned to get even by helping himself to one of the girls in the cage. The oldest was scrappy, with sharp eyes like a hawk. Wally liked that. He had lost his chance with Lola, he deserved this.

★

After Joe and Lola rode off on the motorcycle, Vern sat in the cool dim bar thinking about his life and when he was wounded in Korea. They had shipped him to a military hospital in Boston. Those days were still a blur. Before his one eye opened someone spoke his name. "Vern, Vern are you awake?" A voice asked. "Ya, should I be?" He growled. "Where the hell am I?" He struggled to turn over.

"You are in a Indiana hospital. I'm your nurse. They shipped you here from Boston."

Vern raised up on his elbow and groaned. "Well I'm a mean bastard," he slurred, "so get used to me."

"I can handle you," she giggled inspecting his bandages. "Can I get you anything?" She asked.

"Ya a beer. What do I call you, nurse or hey you?"

"Call me Zoe," she chuckled.

"That's a funny name." He coughed. "What did I lose?"

"Sorry to say soldier, you lost your right eye and left leg. I see your name is Vern." She studied a sheet of information. "Between us both you are going to get well and out of here!"

Vern recalled how her gentle voice calmed his pain. She often came into his room after her shift to talk.

After four months of intense pain, suffering and strenuous rehabilitation, Vern and Zoe had fallen in love.

Vern went home with the promise Zoe would follow when her job at the hospital ended.

With friends bidding her goodbye, Zoe climbed aboard a Grey Hound bus. They were married by a justice of the peace in a town not far from the Wabash River. Vern in his Army uniform, Zoe in a filmy white dress.

Zoe crept behind and put her arms around Vern. They kissed long and sultry.

"I was just thinking about us and what a lucky man I am." He whispered in her ear.

"I'm the lucky one." She smiled. Zoe often said "Honest to God, it was love at first sight."

★

Back at the bog sale Joe and Lola were amazed by the crowds of people eating and buying odd things from the venders. Joe estimated three hundred milling about, city folks as well as vagrants. He sent inconspicuous gestures to Lola, like a baseball coach signaling his players. She never spoke, just watched for his instructions. They parked the motorcycle under a huge sycamore. For two hours Lola searched the crowd for Fish Eyes. Suddenly she kicked Joe's foot to indicate she spied him. "He's alive!" Lola felt sick. He was alive, laughing and flirting with a group of young girls. Lola hunched down, she felt numb, even cold in this heat. She had to look twice, was it really him? His face looked puffy. His belly hung over the top of his pants. After Lola heard his voice she was certain it was him.

Feeling unsteady she leaned against a sturdy booth, filled with watermelons. A sign noted "Indiana's finest, long striped, cool to the touch melons.

Under heavy boys clothing Lola could feel sweat running down between her breasts. Fish Eyes looked so at home, happy, roly-poly. Obviously she was the last thing on his mind. It appeared he had no desire to leave.

"That yer bike?" Fish grunted to Joe.

"Ya, she's a fine one, he nodded.

"Why does yer buddy dress so funny?" He sneered. Don't he know its summer?"

"How do I know?" Joe growled.

Fish moved closer to Lola. "Smells like somebody I used to know, my old girl."

"Everything here smells like goat shit to me, "Joe remarked kicking the gravel.

Fish Eyes walked around to admire the shiny blue motorcycle again. "Where ya from?" he asked.

Down by Indy," Joe lied. Lola backed up against the tree for support. She felt dizzy. The shock of seeing Fish alive and the heat from the heavy boy's clothing caused her to feel faint.

Every time Fish walked near the boy he smelled Lola's perfume. "Who's this guy?" He pointed at Lola.

"I told ya once, my sidekick." Joe appeared annoyed.

Fish looked puzzled, he squinted, their eyes met. She knew she didn't care for him in any way, since he chose to join up with these horrible people. It appeared he had never looked for her. Frank was so right. In a split second Fish yanked the boy's arm. Joe stepped in and firmly removed it off Lola. Her throat went dry.

"What's up buddy?" Joe's face went red.

Fish leaned closer to Lola's face.

"What's your problem Pal?" Joe stared him down. I could whip you with one arm."

"Come on kid, let's get something cold to drink." Joe started pushing the bike away.

"My old girlfriend smelled like that." Fish yelled scratching his long greasy hair. "She died out there in the swamp. Sometimes I can still smell her."

"Could be anybody here." Joe kept moving. "Let's go I'm dry!"

Fish started to follow then walked away.

Somewhere a radio was playing.

Joe and Lola watched two men with pistols shooting into bales of straw. Women wearing cotton dresses and white anklets held their ears as they passed by.

After finishing their lemonade they went to look for the truck. Lola hoped to find the satchel containing her belongings. It would be nice to have her own clothes again.

Lola looked at Joe, what had she ever seen in Fish Eyes. He was a real loser, just like her brother Frank had said. Joe was a strong, intelligent gentleman. She truly felt the fool, although being a foolish girl it had led her to meet Joe, Vern and family.

Lola followed as he pushed the motorcycle among swarms of people. "I'm not used to this hard work," Joe wheezed. While he rested Lola spoke softly in his ear. "We need to find the cage 'cause that's where the truck was before they caught us down the lane."

Joe motioned for her to get back on. They drove in and out of strolling crowds until reaching the lanes entrance.

Suddenly Mr. Gillie came roaring in on his old Harley with Wally clinging on the back. Without regards for the shoppers he spun around in circles, hurling sand and gravel. Lola could hear his evil laughter. Wally slapped the big man on his back as they sped away toward the trailers.

Lola strained to find the truck. "Look!" over there, under those low branches!" She tugged Joe's arm and pointed. "I think I see I see the top!"

Joe nodded and began pushing the motorcycle in the direction she indicated. Sweat zigzagged down his face. His damp shirt stuck to his skin.

The truck was parked in the same spot as before. Dust and dead grass covered the roof and windows. Behind in the shadows stood the horrifying cage concealed under a canopy of low branches.

For a moment the pair stared in disbelief at three little girls huddled in a pile of rags. When the older one peeked out their eyes met. Her thin arms protecting the smaller ones. Wind blew sand between the bars.

"OH God!" Is this real?" Lola gasped. She saw a new rope holding the door shut, just like when she was a prisoner.

"What'll we do?" She groaned. Joe looked stunned." We got to get help. This is too big for us to handle." His voice sounded raspy.

The piteous children looked up with red swollen eyes but never spoke. Their hair was matted, scabs from insect bites covered their frail bodies.

Lola brushed a spot of dust off the truck window. The keys hung in the ignition.

"Don't open the door now, we need to get the sheriff!"

When Joe started the motorcycle Lola struggled to

climb on. She could see swarms of flies covering a plate of food that had been placed inside the cage.

Lola waved a weak hand at the little girls, then buried her face in Joe's back and sobbed.

They roared toward home, leaving mobs of rowdy people to dance and drink the steamy night away.

Reaching the highway Lola's hat blew off and floated behind, her long blond hair streaming in the wind. She removed the heavy boy's shirt and let it sail away.

Joe pulled close to the tavern door. Vern and Zoe hurried out to hear details of their escapade. Lola hopped off and wiped her eyes!" He's alive and well. He never knew who I was. The truck is there. I don't think it's ever been moved. I was so scared."

This is serious, Vern. We need to call the sheriff. I don't think the ordinary shopper has any idea what's going on back there. It looks real bad." Joe pushed his bike into the garage. "We found the truck and three pitiful little girls locked in that cage. We have to hurry! God only knows what they got planned for èm. We need to rescue those girls tonight!"

★

The Sunday sun was sinking in the west by the time Sheriff Payne assembled his posse at the tavern parking lot. The men answered as he called their names.

"Jon!" "Here." "Noah!" "Here." "Bailey!" "Here." "David!" "Here." "Charles!" "Here." "You brought yer dog didn't ya?"

"Sure did!" Charles replied. Just then two County Policemen drove up in their squad cars to join the rescue.

"I'm going too!" Lola spoke up. These little girls might remember seeing me, even if I looked like a boy."

"Alright, you stick close, better tie up your hair. Might get it caught in the branches." The sheriff replied. Once we get our hands on those kids we will bring èm back here. Vern you have an ambulance waiting. I don't care how long it takes. We don't know what we might get help up with. You guys park alongside the highway, don't drive in. Face all vehicles this way so we have a fast getaway.

"Joe and Lola drive Vern's truck slowly directly to the cage. We'll be in the woods watching. Do your best not to let anyone at the sale know what's going on. I'll die before I let those perverts get èm!"

The sheriff wiped his nose. He took off his hat and swiped a handkerchief over his bald head, put it back on and repeated. "Joe, Lola drive Vern's truck straight to the cage. You got a sharp knife to cut the rope? When you get èm out head back here fast! We will worry about getting Fish Eyes truck sometime later. Let's get started. God help us!"

★

No one noticed when Joe and Lola parked near the cage. Lola jumped out and began cutting the rope that held the door shut. She spoke softly to the girls. "We are going to get you out of this awful place."

"Hurry up it's getting dark!" Joe whispered.

The three little girls stood holding hands, watching without speaking as Lola carefully opened the squeaking door. Like a flash of summer lightening, before Joe or Lola could respond the girls ran like the wind, slipping out of sight deep into the forest. Joe and Lola were dumbfounded. Lola cried, "You take the truck back to the highway! Tell the sheriff what happened! I'm going in after èm!" She quickly disappeared into the underbrush.

Joe was swift to catch up with the posse and told them what had taken place.

Sheriff shouted! "Men fan out and head north!" Charles took the leash off Doogie and let him run free.

The men charged ahead without talking. Night

was falling fast. "Where's your dog?" Sheriff called to Charles.

"I can't find him! I hope he didn't go up in that sales area!" Charles felt in his pocket for treats he had brought along for the dog.

In the distance now and then you could hear crazy music and wild laughter.

"Where's Lola?" Sheriff's voice cracked.

"She took off after those kids!" Joe replied. "This is really bad. We'll never find èm now. I'm really worried." Joe whispered.

Just then Lola appeared. Joe rushed over and put his arms around her. "I've been so worried. Did you see any sign of them?" She shook her head, no. "Now we've lost Doogie."

It turned out to be a very dark night. "Why don't we sit down and rest awhile, catch our breath. I'm getting too old for this much excitement." Sheriff slumped down and leaned against a tree. I don't know how long this old body of mine can do this work!" Somewhere in the distance owls called back and forth. Lola had chills remembering Wally speaking about wild hogs in these woods. Noises from the sale area could hardly be heard now.

"What's going to happen when those creeps find out the girls are gone?" Lola sobbed. "Those poor babies, those poor babies!" Her eyes were red and swollen.

Don't cry." Joe whispered. "We'll find them."

★

"Looks like folks are gittin ready to shut down for the night." Fish Eyes yawned.

"Good, hear that thunder, Feels like a storm brewin." Gillie belched. "I think it's about time we boys have a little fun of our own."

"What ya got in mind, Boss?" Wally's face twisted in a devious curl.

"You know boys. It's time for fun. We have waited and worked hard as hell. We deserve a little pleasure. Fish you ready? "I know Wally is." "Depends on what you got in mind." He grunted. "You know dummy!" Have our time. I got some guy gunna buy ém from me tomorrow. No problem just fun and money. I'll split it three ways so we all get some hot fun and money. It's just waiten for us." Gillie grabbed his privates through his sweat pants and shook them at Wally and Fish Eye.

"Wally, go get us some whiskey first. It's been a long day en I'm dry. Nobody will see us do our business right in that good old cage." Mr. Gillie coughed and spit in the grass.

Fish Eyes told himself it would be different alright. He knew it was wrong.

When Wally returned with a bottle the lid had already been removed. He passed it to Gillie, then to Fish and back to himself.

"Pass it around again!" Gillie called. After all three men had drank the bottle appeared empty.

"Wally you go untie the cage rope, me en Fish will be right behind ya." Gillie sucked out the last drop of whiskey. He carefully stood the empty bottle in the grass.

Before Gillie could pick his huge body off the ground Wally was back blurting. "The girls are gone! Somebody's cut that rope to hell! I can't find ém!"

"Shit! I was gunná get three hundred dollars cash each." Gillie cursed and kicked the dirt.

★

A gust of wind seemed to prod the old sheriff with a burst of energy. He got up quickly and said. "Let's find them kids."

Flashlights dotted the woods at the makeshift detail forged ahead. Every now and then a flash of summer lightening lit the forest. Everyone stopped when Sherriff sent out a signal to hold up. "Charles whistle for Doogie, see if he comes back." Several whistles went out. They waited to hear the dog coming through the dry leaves. I guess not, I don't see him. Maybe we can find ém when it's light. Let's stay here en wait for morning.

The makeshift posse and Lola settled, no one spoke. Sheriff checked his gun and blew his nose.

Through the heavy forest a sliver of sunlight peeked. A couple more minutes en we'll move in deeper. I wouldn't think those little ones could get very far. Wonder where that dog of yers went?" Sheriff looked at Charles.

"He's a smart dog, he'll show up sooner or later, Charles replied softly. Let's go, it's plenty light!"

Now and then through the dense foliage you could hear a fellow trip and fall over a rotted log, cursing under his breath. Suddenly they heard a low growl. "Shine a light over there!" Lola called out. To everyone's surprise Doogie was lying against the girls. They held onto his fur. He growled loudly, showing his teeth when approached.

Charles rushed over. "Doogie, good dog. It's ok, we won't hurt them." Doogie wagged his tail, he understood. Charles reached in his pocket and offered him a biscuit. The children appeared too weak and tired to put up any fight.

Lola squatted down. "We came to take care of you. You did good with the dog. He's your friend. We are your friends. Please don't be frightened." Tears of joy rolled down her face as she picked up the smallest child. Joe took the oldest and Noah lifted the middle one.

Sheriff whispered "Thank you Jesus." Jon, you run ahead, warm up your vehicle. We'll be right behind you."

The tavern was well lit and cozy when the posse came in carrying the little girls. Vern and Zoe held the door open. "Good job you guys." Vern patted their backs as they entered. "Get washed up, foods warming."

"Let Doogie in, he deserves a lot. We found that dog huddled smack dab against those kids." Sheriff smiled broadly.

Joe came from the kitchen with warm coca for each girl. Carefully he held the cups for them. "Who are you?" He spoke softly to the oldest one. She hid her face with her hands and peeked through her fingers, I'm Carrie."

"Are these your sisters?"

"No." She breathed. "Man took us from school yard. Said teacher wanted us. We never got to see teacher."

Lola was moved watching how gentle Joe was.

"We are sending them to the hospital. Doctor's is going to check over ém, see to those nasty bug bites."

The sheriff told Vern. "State Police are working on the missing children report."

"I'm going with them." Lola stood by the ambulance as the medics carried them out.

"Joe, come get me when I call." He grabbed her hand and gently kissed her mouth.

It was well after ten o'clock in the morning by the time all the men from the posse finished eating breakfast and left.

Returning from the hospital Joe and Lola hurried inside the tavern to ready themselves for the expected lunch crowd.

Lola could hardly fathom what had taken place all night until now. Most clear in her mind was the soft kiss Joe had placed on her lips.

Joe chuckled to himself as he heard someone say to Vern, "You sure eat fast, like you are going to catch a train."

"Ya, guess I do." Vern answered. "Think it's from those Army days. Eat now, get blowed up later." His eyes wert dark remembering.

Sheriff caught Joe's arm as he brought clean dishes out to the salad bar. I think you and the girl should go back to the bog and get that truck for her tonight before they get on to us. State Police will be raiding soon." Joe nodded.

"No!" Sheriff changed his mind. "Better get Charles to go with you instead of Lola in case there's trouble gettín it going. Charles is a whiz, he can make anything run."

★

"Who'd ya think took ém?" Wally wheezed.

"Don't know but aim to find out." Gillie finished his breakfast, shoved his dish toward a woman to clear it away.

Fish Eyes came running up, out of breath. He blurts. "My truck is gone! My truck is gone! The girls, are gone, now my truck. I bet somebody took those girls, put ém in my truck and drove away. That was my truck!" He wailed.

"Oh, suck it up. Those kids were money in my pocket. Shit, we really got screwed." Gillie cursed. "No fun for us – no truck for you." He got up from the picnic table and disappeared inside the trailer.

"Well, how'd you like that?" Fish stared at Wally. "He don't give a crap I lost my truck. I can't even report it stolen to the police."

Wally shrugged. "Shit happens. Give it a rest."

Deep down inside Fish Eyes felt relieved the girls were gone. He had had a strong pull to take a girl. If they had not been missing when the time came, he knew he would have gone along with those guys.

★

The Drunkin' Monkey did his neon rotations on top the tavern while folks inside were enjoying a quick breakfast or an early lunch.

As Lola greeted an older couple and took their order, she felt on top of the world with her life now. After giving their order to Joe, she chatted a minute. "What brings you folks out this sunny morning?" Lola smiled.

"We came to catch that big sale going on up the road. I like to look at all the stuff." The woman beamed. "I got this purse there last year. It's held up good." She lifted a gaudy sack for Lola to see.

"Ya, she gawks at everything. I just sit and watch the people." The old man took a gulp of coffee.

"What's yer name girlie?"

"I'm Lola." She pointed to her name tag.

"How long ya worked here?" He asked.

"Not very long." She topped off their coffee.

"You live around here?" He questioned.

"I'm really from Three Oaks, Michigan."

"That's quite a ways. How'd you come this way?" He looked puzzled.

"Oh, that's a long story." She laughed. "I see your order is up."

After leaving the old man called. "Thanks, Lola, it was good food." She waved as they walked out the door.

After parking at the big sale the old lady went straight to a booth of handmade jewelry, spending one hour inspecting each piece, before buying a ring made out of colored wires.

Fish Eyes was still angry that his truck was gone, and walked back to the spot it had sat. Only thing visible was a large patch of dried grass and where someone had brushed dead leave and limbs off the hood and windshield.

Sadly he walked back and flopped against a tree to watch; the crowd and hide from Wally and Mr. Gillie, whom had taken the loss of his truck far too lightly.

"Hi sonny," the old man looked at Fish Eyes.

"Hi yerself," he grumbled. It was obvious he had been drinking. He slurred and fidgeted.

"You don't look very happy sonny. This is a happy place, don't ya think? My wife is over there blowén her Social Security check. I'm the one who ought to look sad!" The old man laughed. "Two things she likes best is diamonds and good perfume. I never gave her any. I call her my old radish – she still has a little zip left in her. Guess I'm used to her, been married fifty years. A woman can walk all over ya and you can still be nuts about her." The scent of fresh cut hay floated overhead.

"Ya, I was nuts about a girl once." Fish mumbled.

"What she do, dump ya?" He asked.

"No, I guess she died. Her name was Lola." He made circles in the dirt with a stick as he spoke.

"Lola, we just met a girl named Lola. Ya don't hear that name much. Now I've heard it twice today." The old man called to his wife. "Wasn't that girls' name Lola where we ate this morning?"

The old woman shook her head, "yes."

"Honey see these hair combs."

Ya, what about ém? He asked.

"I'd really like a set." She smiled holding up a pair.

"How much they want?" he called.

"Seventy five cents." she answered.

The old man looked at Fish. "My ma always used to say, 'cheap men are boring" as he waved a dollar bill at his wife. "Go ahead Baby, they'll look good in yer hair.

Fish leaned back against the tree. Remembering that Lola wanted to stay in a motel the second night out. If he had not been so cheap and said no. If he had made her happy, maybe they would still be together.

"She was a pretty little thing. Long legs, blond hair, pony tail. A real looker; sweet too."

"Where'd you say you was?" Fish jerked forward.

"We was down the road. That place has a funny monkey on the roof. I tipped her good!" Hey Bud! You know I'm a magician? At home folks love to watch my tricks."

"Ya. Fish growled. "Do magic, make yourself disappear."

"Well crabby, cheat yourself." The old man grunted.

"You say she was a waitress at the tavern." Fish grabbed the old man around the neck and squeezed and shook his head until he was blue.

"Let me go! He cried. "You nuts? You nuts? Let me go!"

"Fish Eyes shoved the old man almost knocking him over.

"What's a matter? I say something wrong?" The old man stammered. "Come on Ma!" he yelled to his wife who was picking through a bushel of patchwork potholders. "Come on, this place is nuts! We're leaving."

Fish jumped up. Dark slits of confusion passed over his face. "I'll kill her if I find out she double-crossed me. That little bitch!"

What's wrong with you?" The old man yelled. Fish didn't answer. He hurried back to the trailers in a daze.

"I just heard something. Some old man and his wife back there said a girl named Lola is waitin tables at that tavern down the road. Described her to a tee!" I gotta go see for myself." Fish looked at Wally.

"You told me she was dead!"

"Ya, I did. I couldn't find her. Thought quicksand got her. No, I didn't see her góin down but what else would ya think?" He sounded defiant.

"You never could tell the truth!" Gillie growled, as he appeared. "Maybe we better go take a look. I bet where ya find the girl you'll find yer truck!"

"Maybe she got them girls out." Wally raised his brow.

"Well, maybe boys we'll have ourselves a bit of fun if it is her. Give her a little hemlock tea if you know what I mean." Gillie got up, coughing and spitting all the way inside the trailer.

★

The next day, driving back from visiting the little girls in the hospital, Joe looked at Lola and said, "You know Lo, I'm getting used to you being around. I'm liking it a lot. Are you really thinking about leaving us and going back home to Michigan?"

"I think I should. I've been here long enough. You people will be getting sick of me and all the drama I've caused." She felt embarrassed.

As they parked at the tavern, Joe became serious. "The only trouble is I've fallen in love with you. I can't stand being away from you very long," he whispered pulling her close. They kissed softly. The second kiss was full of fire.

"How can you love me?" Lola's eyes filled with tears. "I've been so stupid." She rested her head on his chest. "Yes, Joe I do love you too. I've seen how wonderful you are to us all. I really love you."

He held her close all scrunched up in the front seat of his car. "Oh, I've wanted to hold you for a long time. I could hardly wait." Joe breathed. "Do you think you could ever marry me? You know all I know is how to cook." He cupped her face in his hands. "You are so beautiful. I love you so much."

"Yes, I would be proud to marry you. You know all I know is how to be a waitress." They both laughed. I'm so young. I haven't finished high school yet."

"We better get inside. I don't want Vern to think we let him down. Let's keep our secret for a few days." Joe opened the car door.

"I don't know if I can, I'm so happy!" Lola beamed. They exchanged another kiss then hurried inside.

★

The sun was going down, another scorching summer was ending. Air conditioning at the tavern felt good for the patrons enjoying supper. Vern allowed Charles to sneak Doogie in unnoticed under the table to keep cool. Every now and then Charles would slip a treat to the sleepy dog.

Vern looked up from behind the bar when a large, tobacco chewing, greasy looking man bounded in, followed by a smaller, seedy, red faced fellow. They pushed their way up to where Vern was wiping mugs with a soft white cloth.

"Can I help you fellows?" Vern asked.

"Ya, give us some beers." Mr. Gillie snarled.

Without any comment Vern slid two mugs their way. Through the kitchen door Lola came carrying a large dinner tray toward Charles and Noah who were sitting together talking about baling hay.

"That's her!" Wally blurted.

"So it is!" Gillie gulped down the whole drink without stopping, then slammed the mug on the bar.

Through the door Fish Eyes approached them. "I found my truck out back, the money's gone!"

Vern overhead and surmised who they were.

All three men watched Lola until she finished placing food to Charles and Noah. They moved closer.

"If you need anything else just call." She smiled. Quickly turning around she bumped into Mr. Gillie's fat belly. "OH! was her startled cry. The tray dropped.

"OH, yourself." Gillie mimicked. "I think you owe Fish here an explanation." He grabbed her hands. She jerked free and attempted to go to Vern, but was blocked.

"Charles and Noah looked up realizing what was taking place.

"Lola, I've found you! Things I said we'd do, you can ice sake, Baby!" Fish begged. He noticed how much prettier she looked, so refined, so sure of herself. "Baby! Come with me." He stepped closer. Lola's cold stare stuck in his throat like stale cornbread. He swallowed hard. The only thing that moved was his prominent Adam's apple. His once ready smile leaked away. It was obvious he'd lost her.

Fish Eyes yelled. "You took my truck en money!"

"Ya Bitch, you've been a bad girl." Gillie smirked. "You owe him an explanation."

"I don't owe you or anybody else an explanation. Now get out!" Lola stood straight and shouted in his face.

Vern was watching from the bar. He slipped into the kitchen and told Joe to call the sheriff. "Looks like those bog boys are after Lola!"

Vern rushed over and stood near her. "You guys need to leave, you are bothering my customers." Vern tried to steer them toward the door.

"You better give me back my truck keys en money you took!" Fish's face flushed with rage.

"You better come with us!" Mr. Gillie started to pull on Lola's arm. "You need to come with us and give yer old boyfriend back his truck!"

"I'm not going anyplace!" She shouted. The scuffle became serious. Tables were bumped, dishes went crashing to the floor forcing startled patrons to move out of the way.

Wally hung back and eased toward the door when Lola screamed and kicked at Gillie and Fish. Doogie leapt out from under the table and socked his teeth in Gillie's leg. When he let go of Lola to fight off the dog, she ran away.

Quickly Doogie let go of Gillie's leg and viciously bit at Fish Eyes back side, ripping open his thin pants, tearing flesh from his buttocks.

Just as the Sheriff came flying through the door Mr. Gillie shot Doogie. The dog yelped and fell to the floor. With one heavy blow, Charles knocked Gillie to his knees. Snot and blood hung from his nose. His blubbery jowls wobbled. His gun fell out of his hand as he slumped to the floor. Charles picked it up and stuck it in his belt. Noah had slipped away when he spied Wally sneaking toward the door for a fast getaway. Noah grabbed Wally before he could escape, and twisted his arms behind his back in a painful position.

In the distance they could hear State Police sirens approaching.

When Fish Eyes stood up his buttock were exposed, bleeding profusely where Doogie had torn out chunks of flesh, his face went pale, he fainted.

While police handcuffed the three felons, Charles lifted the big dog off the floor and held him close. "Vern, call the vet for me, tell him I'm bringing my dog. It looks bad, real bad!" Tears were running down the brawny man's face. The faithful dog's blood seeped on his master's pink shirt.

"I bet now we will find out where those little girls came from, Joe comforted Lola in his arms.

Patrons milled about wondering what had just taken place, and what it all meant.

As the last customer left Vern locked the door and shut off the neon monkey's lights and placed a closed sign in the window.

★

After Vern and Zoe disappeared upstairs, Lola still

could not calm down after the day's horrid events. Out her window she saw a full moon. The air had not cooled, she felt sticky and nervous. Dressing in clean shorts and a loose shirt, she slipped out into the back yard. Night bugs chirped; the grass felt cool on her toes. Lola turned on the hose and let the water run over her body, through her hair, down her back, up under her breasts. The cold water soothed her throbbing head. Lola jumped as Joe's arms went around her small waist.

"You scared me! I'm so glad it's you," she smiled. Joe let the hose wet his chest and back. They stood under the running water without talking. Their lips met, warm and wet. He tipped her face, they kissed again and again. Their wet young bodies stuck together.

Joe reached down and shut off the water. They sat on the grass all cool and clean.

"Baby, I need you. Please don't say you are going back to Michigan. I can't bear the thought of us not being together. I love you."

"I love you too," Lola sighed. She touched his hand.

"I don't think you should leave anyway. The court will need you to testify against that bunch."

"I suppose so," she thought. "I do need to get out on my own." She tucked her hair behind her ear.

"Why not get out on your own with me?" Joe laid

gently back on the wet grass. He rolled on his side and pulled her cool body close to his. 'Baby, I'm suffering, I need you bad. You are all I want." His arms felt strong, his kisses soft and sensuous on hers. Their wet bodies pressed together.

"Even with all my craziness?" She sighed.

"Even with all your craziness," he whispered. "I've been infatuated with a girl now and then, but never in love like I am with you." Their lips met hard and full of fire.

"Could this be mine?" He squeezed her arm.

"Yes, this is yours." Lola breathed.

"Let's go in my house and dry off." Joe pulled her to her feet. She stood brushing loose grass of her legs.

As they stepped into the cottage Joe reached back and hooked the screen door. Nothing was heard except nigh birds and an orchestra of summer bugs.

It was almost daylight when Lola fell into her own bed. They had talked all night. She asked herself what it is about Joe that has made such an impact on her life in such a short time. This impact she felt would remain for the rest of her life.

★

News of Doggie's recovery spread fast among those

people who enjoyed the food and comradery at the Drunken Monkey tavern. The veterinarian felt he had healed enough to go home. Vern and Zoe advertised to make his come-back a festive occasion. Drinks and appetizers were on the house. Supper meals were ordered.

The parking lot was jammed full when Charles led Doogie into the airy room. The big dog wobbled from weakness but his tail wagged constantly. A large bandage was secured around his mid-section.

Vern yelled to Joe in the kitchen. "Cook up a hamburg- no onions. Our hero has arrived." Everyone clapped and hooted. A banjo player began playing "Back Home in Indiana." Feel free to pet the hero," Vern shouted.

As Lola hurried down the stairs, Vern tapped on a glass for the crowd to quiet down. "Joe says he has something to say." The groups went silent as Zoe came inside carrying Chickie who was sporting a new sun bonnet. "OK, Joe what's on your mind? Spill it." Vern prodded.

"Hey, Lo get over where you can hear better, stand by me." Joe called. She walked closer feeling a little awkward.

"Friends, I want you to be a witness when I ask Lola to marry me." He reached for her hand. "Lola my dear, will you marry me?" Her face took on a surprised, angelic smile.

"Yes, Joe I would love to marry you." Taking a diamond from his pocket he slipped the engagement ring on her finger. When he pulled her close the crowd went wild. Men shouted and raised their mugs. Women took out tissues and wiped their eyes.

"When you getting hitched?" Someone shouted.

Joe looked at Lola and asked, "When"?

Her answer was "soon."

As the crown settled down, Sheriff motioned to Vern and Joe to come over by him and all the men of the posse.

"I was telling the boys we need to go back to the bog, since tomorrow is their last sale day. We need to snoop around now that those three ones are locked up. We gotta find out who was responsible for those little girls. I'd love to get my hands on those bastards. Let's snoop tonight and tomorrow, then meet back here after church Sunday."

"We will cook breakfast for everyone when you get back," Vern and Joe added.

"Since I'm sheriff I'm going to do my best to close that place down for good."

★

As men from the posse drifted about the sale area they noticed some venders appeared to begin packing up.

"You leaving?" Noah asked at the watermelon booth.

"Ya. I've practically given them away. I don't want to haul ém home. I cut the price in half."

"You coming back next year?" Noah angled.

"I might if I get a decent crop next summer. I ain't seen those guys in charge for a couple days to sign up again. I'd hate to pay for a spot to hold for next time. Have you seen ém?"

"No, I don't know who they are." Noah lied.

"You can't miss ém. What a bunch of misfits. Guess I'll pack up and head home."

Sheriff ambled over by the trailers. A small boy was playing with a broken toy car in the sand.

"Hi, sonny," Sheriff greeted. "What's your name?"

"Henry, Ma calls me Hen." He kept looking down.

"Is your mother home?"

"Ya, she's cookin," he shucked his head toward the nicest looking trailer.

"Your dad home?" Sheriff pried.

"Ma don't know where he went."

"Can I talk to her?"

"She don't know you." The boy looked up.

"I know, but maybe I know where your dad is, will you get her?'

The boy jumped up, pushed his face against the screened door and yells, "Ma some guy wants ya!" A muffled voice spouting cuss words leaked out.

"Ya." An unpleasant woman appeared at the door. Her hair looked like a mass of dirty cotton.

"Ma'am, I want to speak to your husband. I think his name is Mr. Gillie.

"You'll have to find him. I ain't seen him." She handed the boy a cob of sweet corn then retreated back inside. With sandy hands the boy began turning the cob over his lips.

As the sheriff turned to go he asked, 'Say sonny, what ya have in that big cage back there, bears, lions?"

"If you be bad my dad'l put ya in it." A dark expression swept his small face.

"Did he ever put you in it?"

The boy shook his head. "Not me, but I saw some girls once."

"Do you think they were bad?" Sheriff spoke softly. Henry shrugged and continued digging in the dirt.

Vern and Joe had a Sunday brunch ready when the sheriff and his men arrived back from spying out the sale grounds. All agreed they had met some really seedy looking characters, but also some legitimate shoppers.

"I'll go back in a few days and see if people are still living in those old trailers. We need to get all those squatters out of there. We have a whole year to shut it down, if that's what it takes. I need to check with the police at the jail to see what's with those three prisoners." Sheriff Payne thanked Vern for the food and his posse for all their help.

★

Red sumac and goldenrod bobbed like fairy dancers in the early fall breeze. Trucks carrying tomatoes to the cannery passed daily. Tractors roared past The Drunken Monkey piled high with bales of sweet smelling hay. Often a driver would stop in for a cold drink and a sandwich.

Later in the day Vern called to Lola. "Better get anything you want out of that truck, Sheriff's sending a tow truck to haul it away. I'll be glad to see it go out of here, it's nothing but bad memories."

Lola felt happy about her life now. She could not wait to tell her mother. She hummed a catchy tune as she crawled up under the truck cap. Quickly she stuffed her wrinkled and dusty belongings into the satchel.

To her surprise the truck door slammed, motor turned over and pulled out of the parking lot at a high speed. Lola fell against the side as it jolted upon the highway. Pulling herself up she could see through the small window the back of Fish Eyes' head. Lola screamed and beat on the glass. He raised his hand as if to greet her as they raced up the road. He turned down the bog lane, over the ruts and broken limbs the truck bounced, then jerked to an abrupt stop behind the steel cage area.

Fish Eyes jumped out, then opened the back where Lola cowered. Her head was bleeding where she had smashed it against the back panel.

Fish grabbed her arm attempting to drag her out. Lola screamed and kicked at him. She tasted blood in her mouth like a freshly pulled tooth.

"Come on now! Settle down. I won't hurt you. Don't you remember yer my girl? I found ya baby! We'll do all those things ya wanted to do now. Come on let me help ya outa there."

Lola moved closer to the tailgate, ready to slip off. "Let me alone, I can get out myself." Her cold stared fixed. "I thought you were in jail." She cocked her head and wiped her bloody mouth. Her erratic heart beat in her chest like a clock pendulum off kilter. She drew in a mouthful of air like a desperate fish sucking in water. Lola could hear the cage door swinging in the wind.

"Well here's where two fools meet." She smarted and tried to appear calm. All the time he noticed how pretty she looked even tho her face and hair was a mess.

"Ya, I was in jail." Fish stepped closer, she could smell his reeking breath. Shards of sunlight crossed his face. "You're the fool not me," he growled.

"Baby, come to me. Don't be scared. Remember how happy we were?"

Lola began to cry. Her tears tore him apart. He had been so sure she would run to him crying with happiness. They would slip away from all this chaos and be happy ever after. His nectarous words made her sick.

"You double-crossed me! You didn't stick up for me!" He gritted his teeth and glared. "You let me down. If you'd done what they wanted I wouldn't be in all this shit!" He dropped his cigarette and ground it in the dirt with his shoe.

"How could I help you! Wally was dragging me away. You never tried to save me!" She shouted. "What about those little girls?" Lola cried out, "what about them?" Foam began foaming around his mouth, exposing his unstable nature.

"You locked them up didn't you?" She glared,

"What if I did! We never got to ém" His eyes

narrowed. "You! It was you!" He knew he had outrun his secret.

"Well it's time for me. You turned me down before, but ya can't now!" His yellow teeth showed through a lecherous smile.

"I'm engaged now." Lola held up her ring finger.

"You'r goin to marry that dumb cook? I remember you tellin me you were savin' yerself for when you get married. Well, I'll just fix that. "I'll be havin' you first!"

Fish began dragging her into the woods. "Scream all you want, nobody's here to hear ya!"

Every time Lola attempted to run, he knocked her down.

As fish struggled to pull out his erect penis, he had to strike her again and again. Sprawled in the leaves stunned and bleeding, Lola groaned. As Fish Eyes dropped his pants, he wheezed. "savin' yerself huh?" In a state of frenzy he tore away her blouse.

Closing his eyes Fish positioned himself for his reward. Regaining her senses, Lola reached for the satchel, frantically she was able to pull out an ice skate. With uncanny strength she thrust the runner's pointed blade deep into his hanging testicles ripping open the soft sac. Fighting hard to control her unsteady arms, she pulled back and jabbed the blade in his face and eyes.

He howled in pain. With the last bit of her strength Lola stabbed the blade point tearing his testicles for the second time.

Struggling, Lola wrenched free from under his bleeding body.

"I'll kill ya!" "I'll kill ya!" His demonic screams echoed through the trees.

Lola didn't notice the ragged clouds, or feel rain pelting down as she stumbled toward the truck.

Fish Eyes staggered behind with twisted pants around his ankles. Blood dripping from his face and privates. He screamed death threats.

Fortunately the truck started on the first attempt. Lola shifted and swung it around before he reached her. In the rear view mirror she saw him fall down in the lane.

When Lola pulled up and out on the highway a fast moving semi slammed the truck broadside, hurling her deep into the ditch. The back wheels spun around hitting a rock, making a noise like someone tapping down a fence post.

★

At the tavern Vern strolled over to answer a ringing telephone.

"Vern, hear this." The Sheriff shouted. "I just got word one of those prisoners has escaped!"

"Which one?" Vern asked.

"I don't know, I'll find out and call you back."

"Thanks Sheriff!" He hung up and yelled. "Joe, Zoe go get Lola. She's cleaning out the truck! One of those bad guys escaped!"

Joe ran out the front door, looked about then ran to the back of the tavern.

"Call upstairs for Lola," he shouted. "There's no truck out here, maybe they hauled it away already!"

"No, I don't think so, somebody would have told me. Zoe, look in her room, in the shower!"

Joe ran to look in his cottage, calling her name. Frantically they met. "We can't find her. I even looked in the basement!" Zoe began to cry.

Vern quickly dialed the Sheriff. "We can't find Lola, and Joe can't find the truck. Did you find out which guy escaped?"

"Yes, it was Fish Eyes! I'm coming!" Vern heard the telephone slammed down. "Where do we look? What will we do? I'm so scared for Lo!" Zoe shivered.

The sky turned a greyish blue, a drizzling rain pestered. Just then they noticed cars backed up on the highway east of the tavern. County patrol cars raced by with sirens blaring. Close behind came an ambulance.

Joe jumped on his motorcycle and weaved around and through waiting vehicles. When his eyes and his brain put the scene in front of him together, he realized it was the notorious missing truck. It lay on its side, severely caved in, windshield shattered. Medics and policemen were struggling to pry open the door. Joe heard one say "It's a woman." Another asked, "Is she alive?" He squeezed his way past, shouting, "Is it my girl?" Fear gripped his chest. His blue eyes glazed with questions. His ruddy complexion turned pallid.

"Is she breathing?" Is she alive?" He kept pushing closer and screaming questions.

"Stay back buddy, we got to help her!"

"Lola! Lola!" Joe could tell it was her. "That's my girl!"

"Back away, we will get her."

Joe backed away as they pulled Lola out of the wreckage, and placed her on a stretcher. Her face was covered with blood, she moaned. "That's a good sign." Someone spoke as they labored up the embankment. Once on the highway Sheriff bent close to her face. "Lola, who? Why?" "Fish" she breathed.

"I'm here baby! I'm here!" Joe spoke loudly. Their eyes met momentarily. Then she passed out.

"Joe, you go with her!" Sheriff checked his gun. Briefly he explained the situation to the officers. "I'll tell Vern to wait for any incoming calls that might come in!" Sheriff shouted as Joe was getting into the ambulance.

The semi driver approached, all shaking and frightened. "Honest to God! That truck pulled right in front of me. I couldn't stop! It happened so fast!" He wiped his nose and eyes.

"Where'd ya say it pulled out from?" Sheriff asked.

"Over there. Out of that dirt lane!" His quivering finger pointed to the bog entrance.

"That's a good place to look for a scumbag named Fish Eyes." The sheriff shook his head. Taking one last look at the wrecked truck, he noticed ice skates that used to be white, now covered with big splotches of blood drying to sticky smears of brown in the sun.

After Lola was conscious, cleaned up and stabilized, she was able to explain to Joe and police what had happened. Due to the hard bump on her head, the doctor requested to keep her overnight for observation. Both eyes were black, and her right arm was broken.

"Lo, you are my best waitress, you got to get that arm healed. I need you." Jose kissed the top of her head. She could barely smile or nod. He bent close. He could breathe in her breath. "Darling, I was so frightened.

I thought I'd lost you. You are the only one I'll ever love. Get well baby. I need you. We got to get married. I don't ever want to be away from you." Tears rolled down his face. Lola placed her hand on his. He kissed her diamond ring.

"I'll be here tomorrow to take you home."

★

Holding his bloody crotch, Fish Eyes crawled into a cool and quiet trailer. Everyone had gone. Whippoorwills called, a soft wind moaned. He dug around in a cupboard looking for something to drink. The only thing left was a bottle of whisky with no lid.

Tiny streams of blood from his torn scrotum ran down his legs into his dirty shoes.

He thought about Mr. Gillie and Wally still in jail. He recalled how he had escaped, easy as pie. He walked out in the middle of a group of visitors even before he got locked up.

Soon the bottle was empty. He nodded, then fell back on a lumpy mattress, sound asleep.

It was morning, Fish awoke with a start. He thought someone was banging on the door. He sat up, his head was exploding.

"Who's there? Who's there?" He yelled. Slowly he realized it was a loose door on the trailer thrashing in the wind.

Fish stood on the steps and urinated out on the grass. He felt like screaming, it burned like fire down there.

He knew he had a fever. His sac had swollen double in size. His wounded testicles seeped blood, they had stuck to his pants all night. He was mad, he felt betrayed. "That little bitch, I'll kill her!" His guts twisted with hatred. His crotch hurt bad. "I'll grab her skinny neck and squeeze," he growled.

Fish opened a can of pork and beans and ate out of the can. After taking three bites he left it sitting on the table and hobbled outside.

"Guess I'll go snoop in Mr. Gillie's trailer." He mumbled to himself. "See what I can use. I'll look for money." Fish had no idea when Gillie and Wally would get out of jail, so he could take his time. If they did get out they wouldn't be able to pin anything on him. He'd be long gone.

A zephyr breeze ruffled Fish's unruly hair as he entered Gillie's trailer. He hoped there would be something better to eat than those crappy pork and beans he had for breakfast.

It looked to him that the people who lived here had made a fast getaway. A greasy skillet filled with something he could not identify still sat on a cold burner. Dirty clothes were scattered everywhere. Fish spent an hour digging in drawers and closets. He had to sit down several times he felt so weak. His privates hurt, once he almost fainted. The pain between his legs was getting unbearable.

Back in his trailer Fish dumped the contraband on the table to inventory. He counted out enough money to get him far away from here. He sorted his booty and whispered "nice."

Fish locked the door, laid down on a dirty bed with a broken headboard and slept till two.

★

Lola as happy to be home from the hospital. A large soft chair was placed in the dining area so she could greet her friends stopping in for supper. Zoe brought Chickie Pear down to show everyone how she learned to walk. Folks clapped as Chickie pranced about on her new found freedom.

Lola still felt shaky and said good night. "I'll be down early tomorrow," she told Vern. "I can still fold napkins and sort silverware." The next morning as Zoe, Lola and Chickie Pearl came downstairs, "Candy Kisses" vibrated through the dining room from the radio. Vern blew kisses to them as he worked behind the bar.

Joe came out from the kitchen. His long white apron was covered with flour. His large hands were sticky with biscuit dough. They decided to eat breakfast in the tavern instead of the cottage. Zoe needed to wash windows and tidy up the big room.

Joe walked over and kissed Lola only touching her soft lips. Her heart fluttered and he turned and went back in the kitchen to work. "Zoe," Lola sighed. "How can I be so lucky to have such a wonderful man like him?"

"I'd say we both are lucky, you have Joe, I got Vern."

Three o'clock that afternoon the dining room was empty after the lunch crowd. Lola dozed in the big soft chair. She still felt uneasy from the wreck. Vern was out in the back dealing with old grease to be taken away. No one noticed in the shadows as Fish Eyes slipped inside. He stood quietly until his eyes focused after coming in from the bright sunshine. Blood and tears oozed around scabs on his face caused by the ice skate incident. His nose leaked mucus, now and then he wiped it on his bare arm. It hung like cold gravy. His head pounded, he needed a drink.

Looking about he spied Lola dozing.

He felt dizzy, almost blacking out as he stumbled, bumping against a table, waking her with a start. It took a few seconds to realize it was Fish Eyes standing in front of her.

"You screwed up my life, you little bitch, now I'm going to screw up yers!" He spoke through gritted teeth. His toad like face glared.

Lola's stomach knotted. She had lost track where Vern and the others were. She knew they were taking a breather between lunch and supper.

"You think I'm a prick! You think you can walk over me like some old dirty rug! I wanted us to be together! Can you remember when we left Three Oaks?" His complexion resembled cooled oatmeal that had spent too much time in the pan.

"You called me a cheap boyfriend, remember en so did Gillie. Look where that gets you en him! I'm going to kill you and he's in jail!" He shook with rage.

Fish felt for the loaded pistol he had taken from Gillie's trailer.

Lola could not speak. She feared her wonderful life with Joe was about to be cut off. She could see blood from his crotch area seeping through his pants. The zipper on his fly was broken and flapping open. Without underwear the skate had cut deep.

"You think yer so great living here, swell huh!"

Lola's head was spinning. "Now Fish, you go your way and I'll go mine. Just leave so you don't get in any more trouble." Lola's voice quivered.

"I came here to kill ya, and that's what I'm goin to do!"

"You don't need to kill me! What will that get you?" Her words drug over her tongue like soggy wool.

"You took my truck! You took my money!" Evidently he did not know about the wreck. "I think I should git a kiss goodbye for I kill ya. I never got one since we left Three Oaks, you little stingy bitch!"

As he came closer he noticed her arm in a cast. "How'd ya do that?" He looked surprised.

"What's it to you!" She smarted back.

"I've had it with you," he growled. His face turned red and blotchey. Fish sprang ahead. He grabbed her face with both hands, he jabbed his tongue deep inside her mouth, like spearing a carp.

Lola fought, pushing, gagging she hit with her cast and pulled his hair causing him to back away. Her mouth felt dirty. She tried to spit between screams.

Fish stood flashing an evil grin. He wiped his dripping lips. "How'd you like that?" Lola's stomach erupted, her lunch spewed down the front of her white blouse.

Fish pulled a short pistol from his sagging pocked and

waved it under her nose. Lola screamed and screamed, kicking hard her feet smashed into his swollen, bleeding crotch. He bent over and groaned. "I'll kill you! I'll kill you!"

Vern shouted, "Hold it!" Fish spun around. "Don't let this one eye and one leg fool ya, buddy! I was a number one sharp shooter in Korea. I've killed better men than you en they were enemies!"

Fish pointed his gun at Lola and pulled the trigger. Vern's gun fired first. Fish Eyes fell forward on top of Lola in her chair. Instantly with all her might she pushed him off, he rolled to the floor. Her eyes blazed, she squealed, sucked in her breath, stretched, stepping wide over Fish's dead body. Her bare feet slipping through his blood.

Fish's bullet had torn through the back of Lola's chair and lodged in the wall behind.

"Vern, you shot him!" She cried. "You shot him!"

"I had to!" He choked.

Zoe came running from outside, Joe rushed in from the cottage. They stood in shock looking down at Fish's body and at Lola's blood spattered shirt and bare feet.

Vern's gun felt solid and balanced even in his trembling hand. "It was self-defense," he whispered. "It was him or Lo." Zoe put her arms around Vern and gently sat him down. "You did good. You did everything right." She spoke softly. "Thank you Jesus!"

"If I hadn't had this gun behind the bar, our Lo would be dead." He swallowed hard. His eyes filled with tears.

As the medics loaded Fish on a stretcher one commented. "By the looks of him, all the blood loss en stuff doesn't look like he had long for this earth. Looks like blood poison was about to take him"

"Guess he's facing the Lord about now," Zoe whispered.

Sheriff Payne drove in with his siren blasting. He jumped out and shouted, "tell me everything!"

For weeks after, newspaper headlines told about Fish Eyes' death at the Drunken Monkey restaurant. The notorious bog sale and Mr. Gillie's and Wally's pending trials concerning their nefarious activities.

Good news was shared when the three little girls were united with their families. Many people wishing them to be happy again without bad memories.

Lola's arm healed, the cast was removed. She was careful not to overload trays she carried.

Police had contacted Fish Eyes' family. They requested his body be sent home to the local funeral home. He was buried in Forest Lawn Cemetery just south of Three Oaks, Michigan. Few people came. He had finally outrun his devils.

★

At the courthouse the courtroom was crowded. The trial was open to the public. News reporters slipped around taking notes. The air felt cold on Lola's face as she waited for the trial to begin. All month long she dreaded coming face to face with Mr. Gillie and Wally. Joe, Vern and Zoe assured her they would be close by.

Six months had passed since all this drama had taken place. Lola felt so at ease now concerning her parents and Frank. They were in contact often. She promised them she would come visit as soon as the trial was over.

The courtroom quieted as several police officers led the accused in to be seated. Neither one looked up or acted as menacing as before. To Lola they appeared to be two old broken men or at best two forms of Satan. Lola shivered. Joe squeezed her hand as they watched the Judge take his seat.

Several rows behind sat the parents of the three little girls. The Judge felt the children had been through enough so far, and didn't call them to testify.

Sheriff Payne and his makeshift posse of Charlie, David, Jon, Noah and Bailey were seated in the back row near the door.

Lola flinched, her heart raced when the bailiff

called her name. Joe squeezed her hand again as she stood. Quickly, she made her way to the front. She was sworn in, then seated in the witness chair. Oh, how she wanted this over with.

The Judge looked at her and spoke in a gentle voice. "Tell us from the beginning the whole story as best you can."

Lola took a deep breath. She felt so embarrassed to admit how she left her home with Fish Eyes. She told about sleeping in the truck, being taken by Wally through the woods and locked in the cage. Her escape from the bog while Wally was asleep in the grass.

She told how she fought her way up to the main road. How she made it to safety at the Drunkin' Monkey restaurant. Lola became emotional when she spoke of the little girls in that horrible cage and how they ran into the forest.

"Thank you." The Judge turned to her. "You may return to your seat. Facing the bailiff he spoke. "Please call your next witness."

"In a clear voice the bailiff called "Sheriff Payne." His testimony was strong against the duo seated on the left. An officer holding a gun stood straight against the wall. His eyes never left the accused.

Charles stood when the bailiff called his name. He told how his big dog was found snuggled up against the frightened children, and how he growled and showed his teeth when the posse approached. At that point the Judge wiped his nose. Some folks wondered if he had a cold, or did the faithful dog story tug at his emotions.

The morning was well spent with one account after another, all clearly exposing their hideous actions. The last to testify before lunch recess was Vern. He gave his account of why he was forced to shot Fish Eyes. "It was him or Lola, and I certainly wasn't going to let it be her." Vern's lawyer now had to prove to the authorities that Vern had killed Fish Eyes in defense of Lola.

The trial lasted ten days after each defendant was found guilty and sentenced to thirty years in prison. The fact they had held three little girls hostage with devious intentions to do harm, and for a profit. A warrant went out to arrest the mysterious devil man who had schemed to buy the children from Mr. Gillie.

Wally used all his charm for leniency by telling the Judge the man's name and whereabouts. Unfortunately, it didn't help him.

Joe and Lola talked about setting a wedding date. It would be soon. "Let's have it right here in my back yard. Lots of room for lots of people." Joe's eyes sparkled as they scanned a calendar for a date. "Look, what about October nineteenth?" "I'd like that." Lola smiled.

"There will be lots of fall flowers still in bloom. We have warm sunny days left before winter."

They kissed. The date was settled, October nineteenth.

"Does it matter you are older than me? I'm just eighteen and not too smart," she sighed.

Joe smiled, "no way, I hear life goes fast. We best get started. My parents knew each other just six weeks. They have been happy together forty-nine years so far."

"When did you know you were falling in love with me?" Lola asked, her voice lowered.

Joe thought for a moment. "Remember the day you said "feel that, something in the air?" You felt fall coming even before we saw any colored leaves of fall. Loving you was like that. Like the feel of fall, not visible, just a feeling, until now, it's fully here."

"We can see our love can't we? We can feel it. It's now." Lola smiled and shook her head yes.

Joe looked deep into Lola's eyes. "I was ok before you showed up, but there always was an empty hole somewhere deep inside me. Now it's gone because of you. Come let's go tell Vern and Zoe."

★

As Lola got ready for bed she looked in the mirror

and sighed. She could not believe tomorrow she would become Mrs. Joseph Baker. High on a hook hung her wedding gown and veil. Zoe had given her a blue garter. Vern had lent her one of his white handkerchiefs in case she cried. Chickie Pearl's role is to scatter rose petals up the sidewalk before the bride. Vern would walk Lola up to Joe and the minister.

The afternoon of the wedding was sunny and perfect. The last cutting of hay sent a sweet smell drifting over the seated crowd.

Vern had ordered the reception dinner catered. Lola was told there might be a surprise.

"What are you talking about a surprise?" Is Doogie dog going to be Joe's best man?"

"Maybe." Vern teased. "How did you guess? Now you spoiled everything."

The crowd became silent as the Sheriff's son began playing "I Love You Truly" on his violin.

The minister, Joe and best man waited in front. Zoe prodded Chickie Pearl to walk up to Joe. "Sprinkle your flowers like I taught you." Zoe whispered. To their surprise the tiny girl did as she was told. Halfway up she dumped the petals in a pile and swooshed them all about with her tiny hands, picked up the basket and continued up to Joe. The crowd chuckled.

"Let's go," Vern whispered as a bridal march began playing. A gentle breeze rustled Lola's beautiful veil.

Slowly, a large man in a black suit stood, then stepped forward and took Lola's arm. Vern slipped aside. Lola paused, but kept on her way to Joe. Her veil blocked her view. "Who gives this woman?" The minister asked. In a clear voice the man answered. "Her mother and I." A woman stepped up and took Lola's arm.

Lola could not believe what had just taken place. Her parents were here. She found Vern's handkerchief and dabbed her tears.

Joe stepped close to Lola as her mother and father took their seats. He squeezed her hand. The minister began the ceremony. The best man presented Joe the ring.

The vows were repeated. Joe lifted his bride's veil, and they kissed.

As they turned to face the crowd the minister said, "May I present to you, Mr. and Mrs. Joseph Baker. I would also like to introduce Joe's best man to everyone. Lola's brother, Frank." The crowd clapped and whistled while Frank hugged his sister.

As Joe and Lola greeted their guests Lola whispered, "Boy was I wrong about the surprise. I really expected to see Doogie dog up there." It was a joyful day.

"How did you know about today?" Lola could

hardly contain her happiness. "My life was changing so fast I neglected the most important, my family." They hugged and cried.

"Joe and Vern came to us several weeks ago. We have been so excited."

"Mom, Dad, Frank, can you ever forgive me for being so stupid?"

"You are forgiven. There's been a lot of praying since you left. This is just answered prayers, that's all. God works in mysterious ways HIs wonders to perform." Her mother smiled, "and Lola, this is truly a wonder."

"Times up." Vern shouted. "We must go in, let the party begin." We have a wedding to celebrate!"

Food and drinks were served to a happy crowd.

Frank punched Joe playfully on the arm. "You did good my little sister; this Joe is a swell guy. We've been talking for three weeks. He told us everything. I feel so lucky to have him for a brother-in-law. Remember, I told you Fish was no good."

Chickie Pearl tottered up to the bridal table and whined for Joe to pick her up. Lifting her carefully he sat her right on the table. Chickie took a piece of chicken off his plate and wiggled to get down.

Someone shouted, "Joe you're goin to be a great

father." A lady asked Zoe why she calls the baby Chickie.

"When she was born she had a clump of yellow hair sticking up on top her head. I said, hello my little chicken. It's been Chickie ever since." Zoe smiled.

By nine-thirty, the baby was asleep in Zoe's arms. The cake had been cut, presents opened.

As folks were saying 'good night' Charles brought Doogie in to greet Lola and her parents. The big dog took the liberty to lick up some wedding cake that had dropped on the floor. At midnight Vern closed things down. A sliver of moon was the only light as Joe and Lola slipped into the cottage and locked the door behind them.

★

Happy years seemed to fly by as Joe and Lola's life together was one of joy.

Chickie Pearl was growing up fast and asked her parents if they would please drop Chickie and just call her Pearl.

Joe and Lola visited Three Oaks often. Frank had married some girl from church, so when his father died during one of the coldest winters in Michigan, they moved in with Lola's mother.

As hard as they tried, no children came from Joe and Lola's union.

They had complete charge of the restaurant now. The neon monkey had stopped working and had been removed.

After much consideration, Joe and Lola turned the restaurant into a home for young orphaned boys.

The whole building was turned into a dorm. Lola had to get each boy a desk and bed, with a colorful spread. Bright curtains were hung at all the windows. Vern and Zoe's apartment was occupied by a couple who were house parents to the boys.

Joe still did the cooking and baking for the hungry group. Lola greeted the boys when they got off the school bus. It was a happy place.

Joe and Lola purchased the property from Vern and Zoe who now live in Indianapolis. Many years passed for Joe and Lola watching all these boys as they grew up. Watching them grow was a great comfort to them. The years were so full and so busy.

The bog had been sold and turned into a very well kept mobile home park. No stories were ever passed around about what it used to be or what happened there long ago.

The gold old sheriff was gone and a new set of young officers stopped by often. Joe still gave them hot coffee and something sweet. He loved to chat and brag about the boys living there.

After many years, Joe turned the boy's home over to the state. His heart was failing and one day he too was gone and Lola was alone in the cottage.

Lola closed her eyes and let the warm sunshine coming through the window rest upon her face.

Holding Joe's small picture against her heart she felt exhausted from remembering all day. She remembered his arms pulling her close in the night. His soft kisses that never ceased to melt her soul. His blue eyes full of love and sweetness for her. OH, those many years together, not one day felt older than the thrill of those first days long ago.

With memories sweet upon her lips Lola died. Happy in her own house, in her own chair.

The End

Printed in the United States
By Bookmasters